"Don't you want to know why I have changed?"

Rosalie couldn't believe he would let her leave his home without some explanation.

"It's obvious, isn't it?" Don Rafael returned. "Somehow you have discovered that I knew you were an heiress." He smiled sardonically. "So you have decided that was the reason I asked you to marry me and therefore I am despicable."

Rosalie nodded miserably. "I believed you loved me," she whispered.

"And now you're convinced I don't. Then I'll not try to delude you further," he said proudly.

Even as she moved slowly toward the door, her heart went out to him in a surge of longing. Was it possible that she had misjudged him?

OTHER
Harlequin Romances
by ELIZABETH ASHTON

Many of these titles are available at your local bookseller or through the Harlequin Reader Service.

For a free catalogue listing all available Harlequin Romances, send your name and address to:

HARLEQUIN READER SERVICE,
M.P.O. Box 707, Niagara Falls, N.Y. 14302
Canadian address: Stratford, Ontario, Canada N5A 6W2

or use coupon at back of book.

The Willing Hostage

by

ELIZABETH ASHTON

Harlequin Books

TORONTO • LONDON • NEW YORK • AMSTERDAM
SYDNEY • HAMBURG • PARIS

Original hardcover edition published in 1975
by Mills & Boon Limited

ISBN 0-373-02247-6

Harlequin edition published March 1979

Printed in U.S.A.

CHAPTER ONE

THE HOTEL MARQUES DE VALPENZA was *en fête* to celebrate an engagement party. One of the renovated Spanish castles that had been taken over by the government and turned into a *parador*, it had become famous throughout New Castile as a must for visitors to Spain—that is, the ones wealthy enough to afford its astronomical tariff. The last of the Valpenzas, possessing nothing except his moldering home and his title deeds, had been thankful to relinquish his outdated marquisate and retire to a modest villa on the coast.

His castle had been refurbished with skill and care to retain its medieval appearance, plus the necessary modern conveniences. The original tiltyard in its centre had been made into a patio ornamented with potted shrubs and colored tiles, while an elegant fountain lifted a plumed jet. The baronial dining hall had been opened onto it on one side, separated from it by a wrought-iron grille, and the diners at the long refectory tables could view the fountain and the greenery through the delicate whorls of black tracery. Standing on a bare hilltop on the arid plateau of the *meseta*, the hotel had little to offer in the way of surrounding scenery, but the Valpenza was a convenient stopover on the long run from Madrid to Cadiz. So popular had it become that the traveler had to book well in advance to be sure of a vacancy.

It was always full during the season—too full,

thought Rosalie Smith as she helped change the courses throughout the long elaborate meal. She and her brother Philip had been placed there by the agency to which they had applied for a temporary job in Spain. They had always wanted to visit Spain and had not the means to come as tourists; besides, they were both sick of working in a big supermarket and the uncertain English climate. Three months of Spanish sun was a lure they could not resist. Unfortunately the position had been a little disappointing, for they found they were allowed little free time and the surrounding country was not very interesting, a seemingly endless and almost treeless plain, with occasional rocky eminences. There was no town in their immediate vicinity, only a small village and the Castillo de las Aguilas, which frowned at the *parador* across the shallow valley that lay between them.

Las Aguilas had not yet succumbed to the fate of the Valpenza, though rumor said its owner, the Conde Rafael de Santaella, was hard put to retain his ancient stronghold. Infinitely more forbidding than its renovated counterpart, Las Aguilas looked like a fitting home for the eagles it was named after, the whole estate being enclosed by a massive boundary wall, above which the distant towers of the Castillo proper brooded menacingly.

But tonight the future looked brighter for Las Aguilas. Consuelo Nuñez, recently arrived from Peru, where her father had amassed a considerable fortune, was that evening celebrating her engagement to the impecunious Conde, who had met the Peruvians in Madrid. The Nuñez money would restore the crumbling magnificence of the castle, and Miguel Nuñez was willing to overlook the bridegroom's lack of fortune in return for his blue blood, for the South American republican hankered after the old nobility and was dismayed by his daughter's inclination to encourage handsome layabouts. He was anxious to settle her with a husband of his own choosing, and the Santaellas could boast of a pedigree a yard long.

Originally he had wanted to buy Las Aguilas as an investment, and that was how the couple had met. The haughty Conde had soon made it plain that his property was not available for commercial development, and then the dowager Condesa, his widowed mother, had suggested that a union between the two families might be advantageous to both parties. So Señor Nuñez had moved from Madrid to be near the Conde while the nobleman courted his daughter. The Smiths had been working there for a couple of weeks when they arrived. Most of the clientele was composed of British and Americans, for whose benefit Señor Gomez, the manager, had acquired an English-speaking staff.

The impact of the lovely Peruvian girl upon the impressionable Philip Smith had been volcanic. She had huge dark eyes and ebony hair, contrasting with a matt white skin; and she was not above noticing the young waiter, whose fair good looks contrasted with her own coloring and who was unable to disguise the admiration smoldering in his gray eyes. It was not long before Rosalie became aware that something was going on between them.

Her sympathies were all with Consuelo, who, Philip told her, had not been consulted about her marriage, and was afraid of the somber Conde. But there was nothing Philip could do to help her, and with sisterly concern Rosalie begged him not to become involved, for Nuñez and the Conde could make life very unpleasant for him if they discovered that he had dared to make a pass at the beautiful Peruvian.

Tonight Consuelo looked very lovely in a midnight-blue dress that showed up her wonderful skin. Upon her wrist she wore a heavy diamond bracelet, a present from her fiancé. He sat beside her, and as Rosalie previously had glimpsed him only in the distance, she observed him curiously. He had a long narrow face with a straight nose and thin lips that curved satirically. Fine dark eyes were shaded by a falconlike brow and his head was set arrogantly upon his shoulders. His was a stern, proud face, as became a Spanish grandee, and she remembered he was rumored to have sworn he would destroy his Castillo before he would allow it to become a hotel.

His manner toward his *novia*—fiancée—was courteous and cold. No one could imagine that there was any love between the couple, and Rosalie's heart was full of pity for the young bride, who hardly dared to speak to the formidable personage beside her.

"It's a damned shame," Philip whispered to her vehemently, as they stood together in the shadow of a giant archway during a lull in their duties. "It's sheer cruelty to throw that innocent to such a satyr!"

For though Rafael de Santaella was unwed, the servants' gossip credited him with numerous affairs.

"Ssh!" Rosalie glanced over her shoulder. "Be careful no one hears you. There's nothing we can do to prevent it."

"Don't be too sure of that!"

"Phil!" Rosalie glanced at him anxiously, while preserving the immobile attitude necessary for an obsequious waitress. "For heaven's sake don't do anything rash. Remember this is Spain."

"I'm not likely to forget, but there are ways and means, even in Spain."

"But she thinks you're only a waiter."

Philip grinned mischievously. He and Rosalie were twins, and very much alike. Both had wide-spaced gray eyes and regular features, but whereas Philip's hair was straw-colored, Rosalie's was bright brown. The waiter's short-coated jacket and scarlet cummerbund showed off Philip's lithe, slender physique, and he carried himself with an air of dignity. At that moment his eyes held a daredevil glint.

"I told her I was a student," he informed his sister, "and that I had expectations. She knows lots of students do take this sort of work during their vacations. I said I was collecting material for a book on hotel life—it sounds more romantic than admitting a connection with a supermarket."

"How could you deceive the poor girl? You know we never got to college, and as for being an author, Uncle George would throw a fit."

"More to the point if the old miser coughed up some dough," Philip observed bitterly and went to obey a signal for attention.

Rosalie gave a long sigh. Philip was becoming rebellious with his circumstances and tired of waiting for the money that would become his when he was twenty-five. Their father had been the head of a chain of supermarkets called Pas, which represented his initials. Philip Alexander Smith had amassed a fortune, but he had been disgusted by his colleagues' spoiled, indulged offspring, who rarely seemed to make good. He was determined that his own children should be brought up the hard way, without privileges. As soon as they left school they had been made to serve in Pas, starting at the bottom, so that they should know the business from A to Z before they inherited his kingdom. How could they learn better than by day-to-day contact with its customers? Still impervious to their pleas for a better life, he died suddenly from overwork when they were twenty. His money was left in trust for them until they were twenty-five, and his brother George was appointed trustee, with instructions that if they borrowed upon their expectations they were to be disinherited.

Rosalie and Philip bitterly resented this decree, especially Rosalie, who wanted to make a career in art. What little time and meager funds she had she devoted to it. They both tried to convince Uncle George that it was absurd that they, the heirs of the great Pas empire, should be serving as cashiers in the store. Surely he could find a way to make them an allowance from the trust. But Uncle George was adamant; he must respect his brother's wishes, and five years was not a long time to wait.

"Only they happen to be the best years of our lives," Philip had said angrily.

The job in Spain had been taken in a mood of defiance, some two years later, and they half hoped their action would make him realize how desperately bored they were with the supermarket. Rosalie was still hankering after her art and Philip wanted to take up writing. But Uncle George remained uncooperative. As a businessman he was suspicious of anything to do with the arts, and though the twins were no great asset to the staff of Pas it had been their father's wish that they should stay there. Since they insisted upon going to Spain, he could not stop them, but he declared they would be poisoned by oily food, get sunstroke, or be murdered by the semibarbaric people.

He told Rosalie, "If you must persist in this tomfool idea, for heaven's sake don't let on who you are. Rich men's children are preyed upon by kidnappers nowadays, and I don't want to have to part with good money—your money—to get you back again. Luckily ours is one of the most common names in the country, so you're not likely to be connected with Pas, unless you boast about it."

"I certainly wouldn't want to do that," she had told him tartly. She thought he was very ignorant about Spain, which was so popular with English tourists. "As for being recognized, nobody would dream I'm an heiress in the clothes I can afford."

"And a good thing, too!"

"But it's a bit hard, uncle, to be so deprived. After all, we're only young once."

"Youth needs no expensive adornment," he proclaimed sententiously, looking appreciatively at her fresh young face and graceful figure. "And continental food can be fattening if you have the means to indulge. You will be better, and safer, if you're taken for a poor working girl."

Rosalie could have hit him. It was poor consolation to reflect that she would have to wait another three years before she could exercise her good taste in clothes and give herself seriously to her painting.

In spite of the hard work, they had enjoyed their stay at the *parador*—it was a welcome change from their former monotonous employment—until Consuelo Nuñez arrived to cause complications. Philip was finding it harder every day to maintain his pose of a waiter, but he was wise enough to know that a story about wealth eventually coming to him would sound unconvincing, certainly to her father.

Seeing the ardent expression in his eyes as he bent to fill Consuelo's glass, Rosalie wished he would not betray his feelings so obviously, though it would never occur to Señor Nuñez and the girl's noble fiancé that there could be anything between Consuelo and a mere waiter. They made a charming couple, he so blond and debonair, she so darkly handsome. Her eyes were nearly as eloquent as his as she glanced up at him from under her lashes, and Rosalie began to feel uneasy. Young hot blood could be so reckless, and this pair were courting disaster.

Reflecting that she herself was an incipient heiress, she supposed that there might be some sense in the provisions of her father's will, after all. She could travel the breadth of Europe without danger from fortune hunters, unlike the unlucky Consuelo who was being sold to gain an aristocratic connection, though she could not imagine Uncle George daring to try to arrange a marriage for her. But she had half hoped that here in Spain, where no one knew her circumstances, she might find romance and have a passionate love affair with someone who loved her for herself alone. The idea had become almost an obsession with her.

Philip came to rest beside her again and she said out of the corner of her mouth, with a wary eye on the distant headwaiter, "Must you look at Señorita Nuñez with your heart in your eyes? Someone might notice."

"I don't care, as long as she does."

"Phil, you can't be serious about a girl you've never spoken to."

"That's all you know!" He flashed a mischievous glance at her. "Waiters can go where other men fear to tread. She looks gorgeous in her negligée when I take her breakfast up to her."

Rosalie looked at the proud, cold face of Consuelo's betrothed and involuntarily shuddered.

"Do be discreet. The Conde looks capable of anything."

"Except love," Philip returned succinctly.

Then it was time to change the courses, and they hurried to their duties.

As Rosalie offered Rafael de Santaella the cheeseboard, she found herself very close to him. His skin was like old ivory and his hair and long sideburns jet silk. He smelled faintly of leather and expensive tobacco. The hand that indicated his preference was long-fingered and beautifully shaped. He was dressed in a short white jacket and a black cummerbund. The jacket, though spotlessly clean, was a little worn at the seams. On the little finger of one hand was a ring shaped like a serpent with ruby eyes. The harsh planes of his face appealed to the artist in her. She would like to paint him as a *conquistador*, emphasizing the ruthlessness indicated by his firm mouth and the arrogant curve of his nostrils. He fascinated her, even while he slightly repelled her. He was speaking to Señor Nuñez in slow sonorous Spanish while she helped him to cheese, and his voice was deep and musical. Rosalie knew that he regarded her as a piece of animated furniture, and not as a person at all. The uniform for the maids at the hotel was a dark blue dress with white collars and cuffs, with the addition of frilly aprons and Dutch caps when they waited on tables. The costume was becoming to her, emphasizing her clear skin and slightly demure air. Suddenly she became aware that Consuelo was looking at her from the Conde's other side and seeing her as a human being. Their eyes met and the Peruvian girl smiled. In spite of being expected to conduct herself like an automaton, Rosalie smiled back, and the Conde looked up at her, his fine dark eyes staring insolently. In their depths was an expression that caused her to decide that Don Rafael deserved his reputation. He would not be indifferent to a pretty girl, whatever her standing, if he found himself alone with her.

Hastily she moved on to the next diner, feeling oddly disturbed by the Conde's glance and dimly aware that his eyes were following her. Suddenly she resented her lowly position; by rights she should be one of the guests, seated at the long table, wearing a dress as rich and becoming as Consuelo's. If he knew her true status and her prospective fortune, Don Rafael would be paying her deference instead of giving her that insolent appraisal. Then she remembered her uncle's warning: it would be only her fortune that could gain the interest of the haughty Don.

The bracelet on Consuelo's wrist caught the light; the diamonds were very fine ones. It was the traditional gift from her fiancé, and if he could give her such a magnificent token, Rosalie reflected, his finances could not be at such a low ebb, though possibly it was an heirloom that had not yet been pawned. Consuelo seemed to find it heavy, or perhaps she regarded it as a shackle, for she kept moving it on her wrist, and more than once her eyes sought Philip with a beseeching look.

Rosalie hoped no one else had marked their covert glances. A liaison between her brother and the beautiful Peruvian girl could spell only disaster; and Uncle George would never approve of a foreign bride for the heir to the Smith empire, apart from the possible vengeance of the flouted Nuñez and Santaella families.

Though she sympathized with the lovers she could not condone their folly and hoped and prayed that Philip would do nothing rash. She comforted herself by considering that Consuelo would be too well brought up to commit any indiscretion, but as she watched those beautiful, passionate eyes, her comfort was short-lived.

Also present was Teresa de Santaella, the dowager Condesa, who was receiving deferential attention from Miguel Nuñez. She was very like her son, except that her expression was a little more human; her keen dark eyes were observant, and Rosalie wondered wretchedly if she had noticed the direction of Consuelo's glances. Women had a much keener nose for romance than men.

Later there was dancing in the great hall that had once been a stronghold of the Christian knights of Spain in their battles against the Moors. Enlarged and redecorated, it still preserved some of its former atmosphere, with great beams across its high ceiling and copies of old tapestries draping its walls.

Don Rafael did not dance. He sat behind a painted screen deep in conversation with Señor Nuñez, smoking narrow black cigarillos and drinking Spanish wine. Their discussions were all of dowries and settlements and they seemed to have forgotten that the object of their planning was left unchaperoned, for the dowager Condesa had left immediately after dinner.

Rosalie was occupied clearing the remnants of the feast, while the stout good-humored peasant women washed up. Philip should have been in attendance upon the guests. The waiters in their smart short jackets and scarlet cummerbunds threaded through the great room with their trays of drinks balanced on one hand, but he was not among them. Rosalie found an opportunity to peer through a service hatch at the swirling crowd of dancers, most of whom were visitors staying at the hotel, but nowhere could she discern Consuelo's blue dress and the sparkle of her diamonds.

Her absence was explained later, when one of the Spanish maids, Juana, said that the Peruvian girl had retired with a headache and had given orders that on no account was she to be disturbed until she rang. She would probably sleep late the next morning.

"*Madre mia*, she is a lucky one," Juana added. "We cannot sleep late however much our heads ache—and our feet, for that matter." She eased her foot out of its shoe.

"Not so lucky to my thinking," another girl declared. "I would not like to have to marry that cold-looking Don. He is enough to give her a permanent headache!"

"Or heartache," Juana shot a sly look at Rosalie. "We know where her eyes are straying, and it's far away from her *novio*."

Rosalie said quickly, "My brother admires her, naturally, but he would never forget his place and hers."

Juana said solemnly, "Then it is true, Rosa, that the English *hombres* are cold as ice?"

Rosalie wondered how she could check this gossip that was circulating among her colleagues.

"Since my brother is a normal young man—" she began.

Juana cut in with a giggle, "Verily a real man, with a man's desires. I think the Señorita Nuñez knows where they tend. I have heard them talking in her suite."

"For heaven's sake don't broadcast it," Rosalie cried, aghast.

"Me, I would not betray true lovers," Juana said smugly. "But it amazes me that the Señor Conde does not see what goes on under his nose. I would advise our good Felipe to walk warily, for if the Conde did discover, his vengeance would be swift and terrible."

"Why, what could he do?" Rosalie asked anxiously.

But Juana became vague, murmuring that the Santaellas were famed for their vindictive tempers, and Rosalie surmised that her love of drama had exceeded fact. She had no idea in what form retribution would fall, only that she was certain it would fall.

Don Rafael took his leave around midnight, which was early for Spain. Señor Nuñez was driving him home, since his mother had returned in the Santaella vehicle. No doubt the news of his *novia*'s headache had been given to him, and he had offered the appropriate condolences to her father.

Rosalie, who had been dispatched to fetch some aspirin for an ailing American guest, saw him go as she crossed the marble vestibule in pursuit of her errand. Though no longer a very young man, he walked with a feline grace and looked slim and debonair beside the Peruvian's stocky embonpoint. Again his black eyes raked her, as she sought to cross the vestibule unobtrusively. She suspected that he missed nothing of what went on around him, except, it would seem, Consuelo's indiscretions, but possibly his overweening pride would not allow him to suspect that she could be looking amorously at another man.

Rosalie hastened into the great hall where the American awaited her and heard the car start up as the two men went away. Involuntarily she drew a breath of relief. There was something oppressive in the presence of El Conde de las Aguilas.

She shared a bare little room with the two Spanish girls and their nights were all too short. Fortunately the *parador* still respected the siesta, though an autocratic government had tried to declare it illegal, and the girls could have a nap in the afternoons. She was up at an early hour to help prepare the trays for those who preferred to breakfast in their rooms. In the bustle of the big kitchen she did not perceive her brother, but that was unremarkable. Philip had been guilty of oversleeping more than once. She remembered Consuelo's instructions and supposed that without the incentive of waiting upon her, he had succumbed to sloth.

It was a day of blistering heat, and once the sun was above the horizon, the atmosphere became unpleasantly oppressive in the kitchen department, which was not air-conditioned like the guest rooms of the hotel. Beyond the grounds the countryside simmered in the heat haze, bare arid stretches with an occasional drift of olive trees, their leaves drooping in the hot sun. There was no greenery anywhere, the sparse grass lay shriveled to a uniform brown, and the stream that ran through the shallow valley between the hotel and the castle had shrunk to a mere trickle. The high wall surrounding the Castillo de las Aguilas merged with the prevalent dun color of the landscape, but the towers of the main building thrust their rugged strength into the white-hot sky, dominating the surrounding countryside as they had done for centuries. When dusk fell they would fade into the night sky, for though the *parador* looked like a fairy palace with its floodlighting and colored strings of bulbs, its opposite number showed no illumination at all. Nor were there any trees or shrubs surrounding that grim construction.

This morning, those in the hotel grounds were already wilting after their nightly baths. Artesian wells had been sunk to fill the swimming pool and supply the *parador* with water through the months of drought, but that was a luxury not to be found anywhere else within miles.

After lunch, when visitors and hotel alike were sunk in drowsy lethargy, the manager, Señor Gomez, called Rosalie to his office. Philip Smith had not been on duty all day.

"Me, I 'ave doubts about 'im, as soon as I see 'im," he told her in his heavily accented English, "but wiz zo many Inglese and Americano clients, it was well to 'ave zomeone who spek ze tongue better zan my villagers, but 'e 'as been lazy, and now, it zeems, 'e 'as walked out."

Rosalie's reaction was a feeling of relief. Though Philip had broken his contract with Señor Gomez, his departure would prevent any further complications with Señorita Nuñez. Possibly he had gone because he had found the situation unendurable. She was a little hurt that he had not confided in her, but perhaps he thought it would be easier for her if she could plead ignorance of his intentions, since presumably she wished to complete the term of her engagement—so she reasoned, being well aware of the impulsive streak in her brother that caused him to act first and think afterward.

"He may only have taken a day off," she suggested.

"Wiz'out permission? It will not do, Rosa. Of you I 'ave no complaint to make, you are zo conscientious, but wiz 'im it is otherwise. I will not 'ave 'im back 'ere. I send for you because I t'ink you know vat 'e do, but I see you do not even know zat 'e 'as gone."

Rosalie assured him that this was so, that she did not know where Philip was, nor even that he had intended leaving. She apologized for him a little perfunctorily, for she was thinking Señor Gomez had got his money's worth out of him—he had endured long hours of hard labor without much pay.

"If we were not zo busy, I would not regret 'im," Señor Gomez told her. "*Madre mia*, what is it?"

Señor Nuñez had burst into the office without knocking, his usually sleek hair on end, his broad face covered with a sickly pallor.

"My daughter!" he gasped. "She is not in her room, she cannot be found. No one has seen her since last night!"

A dreadful suspicion occurred to Rosalie, but could Philip have really been so crazy?

This much greater calamity diverted attention from the missing waiter, and during the ensuing hullabaloo, Rosalie left the office, noting with relief that no one as yet had connected the two absentees with each other. She hoped they would be well away before anyone did, but could they have gone far? Unless Consuelo had some ready cash available, Philip only had his meager savings, which would not take them any distance.

The police visited the hotel in the early evening, suspecting a kidnapping. Staff and visitors were questioned, the former maintaining a loyal silence about their own surmises, but one of the visitors had noticed Consuelo in earnest conversation with the handsome young waiter in a corner of the garden.

"I thought it odd," she told the policeman, for of course it was a woman. "Since Spanish girls are usually carefully chaperoned, aren't they?"

Rosalie was again questioned, but she insisted that she knew nothing and certainly had no idea where the truants had gone. Privately she surmised that Philip would try to join his mother in Paris, where Mrs. Smith resided comfortably on her widow's jointure. Entirely under Philip Alexander's dominance, she had meekly acquiesced to his eccentric plans for their children's upbringing and saw no reason to alter them now that he was dead; but she had a soft spot for Philip, whom she loved more than her daughter, and Rosalie was sure she would give the young couple shelter. But it was a long and expensive journey to Paris, and it transpired Consuelo had not much money with her and only a few trinkets. Her father took charge of her more valuable jewelry. The police were still inclined to favor the kidnapping theory; they could not believe an English waiter would have the audacity to elope with a Peruvian heiress. That was until Concepción Lejos came back from Madrid to meet their barrage of questions. He owned the one taxi in the village adjoining the *parador*, and he admitted at once that he had driven a *doña* and a *caballero* to the capital during the night. The lady had paid him, and he had overheard the couple talking; they were planning to go out to the airfield after they had transacted some business with "the diamonds." Had the diamonds been stolen?

Señor Nuñez groaned. Consuelo had evidently disposed of her betrothal bracelet to raise the funds for their journey. Since she was of age, actually a few months older than Philip, and had taken the passport he had unwisely left in her keeping, there was nothing he could do. Nevertheless he went rushing off to Madrid, where possibly some hitch had delayed their departure.

When the news filtered through to the staff, as of course it did, Rosalie was shocked. Since Consuelo had broken her engagement she should have returned the bracelet, for strictly speaking it was not her property; that she and Philip were spending the proceeds was distasteful to her. To use the hard-pressed Conde's treasure to finance their elopement showed a heartless disregard of his feelings, and after all, he had done the girl no harm. When Philip came into his inheritance, he should refund its worth—it was the least he could do—but she doubted if her feckless brother would spare a thought for the cold proud man he had so deeply wronged.

The rest of the staff were excited and pleased by this romantic episode, for the Conde was not popular, and it was only Rosalie who gave him any thought. His pride and dignity must have been terribly affronted, and she knew enough of the Spanish character to know he would never forgive nor forget such an insult. Philip and Consuelo would be wise to keep out of Spain, and as long as they did so he would have no means of retaliation, even if he did discover their whereabouts.

She found her eyes were constantly straying toward the castle, while she imagined its owner's reactions. He had not appeared during the police inquiry, leaving the outraged father to instigate the search. Juana reported to her that Dolores Lorca, who worked at the castle, had met her in the village and told her that the Conde had declared he wished to have no further contact with either Miguel Nuñez or his daughter. He had called her bad names, saying he was thankful he had found her out before she had disgraced his name.

This attitude, Rosalie decided, was what he would

adopt to salve his pride, but he would not draw the line at calling Consuelo bad names if an opportunity for revenge presented itself.

That she, as Philip's sister, might be vulnerable never crossed her mind.

CHAPTER TWO

TWO DAYS after the elopement, Señor Gomez sent for
Rosalie again and told her that he thought she had
better leave his employment. As long as she was at the
hotel she would remind his staff of the scandal her
brother's conduct had caused, and he wanted the
whole affair forgotten as quickly as possible. Señor
Nuñez had left for Madrid, from where he was making
futile efforts to trace his daughter, and he would not be
returning. But he was not the only person to be offended. Señor Gomez looked at her meaningly, and Rosalie guessed he was referring to his neighbor the Conde,
whose occasional patronage lent luster to the hotel.

"We cannot afford to estrange zese great ones," he
told her. "I t'ink I 'ave made a big mistake by engag-
ing foreign labor, but I could not foresee what would
'appen. You 'ave repaid me very ill, Rosa."

"But I haven't done anything," Rosalie pointed out
indignantly. "I had nothing to do with it."

"I t'ink you lie," he returned, frowning at her. "And
I do not believe you tell ze police all zat you know, but
I do not wish any 'arm to come to you, you 'ave
worked well for me, so it would be best if you go, and
go at once."

"But who would want to harm me?" Rosalie asked,
surprised.

He gave her a furtive look and shrugged.

"*Quién sabe?*" Then he added forcibly, "Take my

word for it, Rosa, you 'ad better go, and go as quickly as you can."

Plainly he was anxious to be rid of her, so much so that he did not quibble about paying her return fare as she half feared he might. It was in their agreement, but she had only stayed half the stipulated time. He included the balance of her meager salary, and as she was putting the money away in her bag, he said insinuatingly, 'Zere is a bus from ze village at noon. It will be good if you go on it."

"Certainly, if you want me to," she told him briskly. She glanced at him a little wistfully. "*Adiós, señor.*"

"*Adiós, Rosa.*" He turned to his desk, dismissing her from his thoughts as he had done from his premises.

The bus from the village went to a town that boasted a railway station, though only the slow trains stopped there, and they were usually very late. Rosalie foresaw a long tedious journey in the bus, with further delay while she waited for a train, and she had no guarantee of being able to get a seat on a plane. She would probably have to spend a night somewhere, but that might be an adventure. Usually she enjoyed traveling, however uncomfortably, but it would not be pleasant in the excessive heat of a Castilian midsummer.

She packed her few clothes into her one suitcase, which she would have to lug to the village, as Señor Gomez was not providing a car as he had done upon her arrival. She wondered if she should seek out her fellow workers to say goodbye. They would all be busy serving drinks and coffee and she shrank from their curious questions. Dimly she felt she was leaving in disgrace, although she had committed no crime. They would, she was sure, be indignant at her peremptory dismissal, and that would entail reopening the vexed subject of Philip's elopement, of which she was becoming heartily tired.

In the end, she decided to say no farewells and slipped unobtrusively out of a side door to avoid going through the kitchen.

There was a terrace in front of the hotel, shaded by giant umbrellas under which visitors sprawled in various stages of undress on their way to and from the swimming pool. They were enjoying refreshments, and she glimpsed Juana's black head as she moved among them taking their orders.

The relaxed scene and everyone's complete indifference subtly hurt her; she felt outcast and forlorn.

She set off down the dusty road toward the village, reflecting that she was not altogether sorry to be leaving. What she had seen of Spain had been disappointing. She and Philip had planned to pay a visit to the south before they left. Granada and Seville with their Moorish palaces and flamenco were what they'd wished to experience, and they'd worked out what they could afford to do on their earnings; but with her employment cut short Rosalie had not saved enough to go, nor had she any heart for a solitary trip.

The hot Castilian *meseta* looked even more arid than usual as she trudged along the shadeless road in the noonday heat. She seemed to have the whole countryside to herself, for nobody who could avoid it would be on the road at that hour. Noel Coward's jingle reiterated in her weary brain, "Mad dogs and Englishmen go out in the midday sun."

The same applied to Englishwomen. She should have insisted upon waiting until the next day and left in the early-morning cool.

A car passed her in a swirl of dust, the only vehicle she had seen. It pulled up a little way ahead of her and she quickened her steps, hoping that its driver meant to offer her a lift. She would risk accepting it, whoever it was, for never had the village seemed so far away, but as she recognized the man who had descended from it, she checked herself. She could not accept a lift from this man, for it was Don Rafael de Santaella.

He stood in the middle of the road with the obvious intention of intercepting her, and she felt an uneasy qualm, which was succeeded by a return of confidence, for he could not know who she was. Even so, if his intention was the kindly offer of a lift, she must refuse, for she might inadvertently reveal her connection with Philip.

She saw that by daylight he looked younger than when she had seen him at dinner in his formal clothes. Perhaps it was the white shirt he was wearing that made him appear so. The short sleeves and open neck revealed his brown sinewy arms folded across his chest, and his strong throat. She was faintly surprised that he had discarded his jacket—Spaniards were conventional in their attire—but the day was very hot. He did, however, wear a black Cordoban hat, pulled over his eyes, which made him look slightly rakish.

She stopped uncertainly in front of him, a slight almost childish figure in the simple suit she had selected in which to travel. Dark glasses concealed her eyes, and she wore a handkerchief over her hair. She looked like a hundred other tourist girls. Knowing she appeared inconspicuous, she took courage; he was unlikely to remember her as the girl who had waited upon him.

A little nonplussed since he did not speak, she said doubtfully, "*Buenos dias, señor.*"

The Señor merely scowled, black brows descending over night-dark eyes that raked her from head to foot from under his hat brim.

Rosalie glanced at the verge on which she must step to pass him—the narrow road was bad enough—but there the dust lay inches deep. Drawing herself up to her full height, she requested in her faltering Spanish, "Would you be so good as to let me pass? I have a bus to catch."

He smiled at her request, an upward twitch of thin satirical lips, and announced surprisingly, "This is a great piece of luck."

"*Señor?*" She was puzzled.

"So you plan to make your getaway, having accomplished what you came for?" He spoke in English with only a slight accent.

Rosalie set down her case, for it was heavy. So he did know who she was and this interception was deliberate; she supposed he was going to ask more useless questions, and she sighed.

"I can't help you, *señor*. And I don't understand why you've stopped me."

"Then you must be very dim. I am surprised the police have permitted you to depart."

Summoning all her resolution, for there was something in his attitude that made her vaguely uneasy, she said coolly, "Why shouldn't they? I've done nothing."

"Imbeciles!" he exclaimed. "You are the one link with the runaways!"

"But, *señor*, I couldn't tell them anything. My brother didn't confide in me. Believe me, this elopement came as big a surprise to me as it did to everybody else."

"Nonsense! Didn't I intercept the meaning looks

that passed between you under my very nose? *Por Dios*, you are no *criada, señorita*. You came here with that *perro inglés* to steal my bride and my diamonds. That fool Gomez must have been blind to employ you!"

Rosalie glanced at her watch; she did not want to miss her bus—they ran infrequently—and the Conde's accusations were futile and untrue. She said earnestly, "Truly, señor, I regret what has happened as much as you do, but I repeat, I cannot help you. I don't know where they are, and it'll be very inconvenient to miss the bus."

He looked her up and down with his insolent stare.

"I am afraid you must reconcile yourself to letting it go," he told her coldly. "I was coming in search of you, as I had ascertained that you were still at the *parador*. To my good fortune and your misfortune, I have caught you in the act of flight. Will you please to get into my car?"

A trickle of ice seemed to run down Rosalie's spine, as she met his gaze. His hat shaded his haughty features, but there was no mistaking the menace that glittered in his eyes. His slim-hipped figure had the supple strength of steel and she knew that physically she would be no match for him. She threw a quick glance behind her in search of succor, but the road was empty.

"I don't know what you want with me," she began, and he laughed evilly.

"That you will soon find out. The police were too soft with you. Perhaps I can make you tell me the truth."

Vivid pictures of third-degree measures flitted through her mind. The man before her looked completely ruthless and he believed himself to be deeply wronged.

"*Señor*," she began desperately, "It was the truth when I said I didn't know anything. The police believed me, so why can't you?"

"They were taken in by your look of innocent candor, which no doubt you can assume when it suits you, but I am used to women's wiles. You won't fool me." He took a step toward her and seized her wrist in a steely grip. "Don't pretend you were not in the plot."

"There was no plot!"

"Do you think I am a complete simpleton? There was a plot; the three of you hatched it together. They stole off in the night and you remained on guard in case Consuelo's absence was discovered too soon. Naturally you protest your innocence, but do not deny that you are about to join them, and that you know where they are and what they have done with the diamonds."

"I do deny it." In spite of her trepidation, Rosalie laughed. His suppositions were too absurd.

"You are amused because you think you can fool me?" he demanded. "But you will find this is no jest, *señorita*."

"No, it's just a bore," she returned. "You've got a fertile imagination, *señor*, but your deductions are quite incorrect."

He drew a quick breath, and a gleam of something like admiration showed in his eyes.

"You are no weakling, *señorita*," he admitted, "though, you may be shameless. But if you will not tell me what I want to know, I have no alternative but to continue to delay you."

Rosalie was almost certain that if they had procured

funds, Philip would have taken Consuelo to Paris, in which case they would be out of Don Rafael's reach, so there could be no great harm in telling him that. But he might insist that she reveal her mother's address, and then their identities would be discovered. Philip Alexander's widow had settled into comfortable anonymity in an apartment there, and both she and Uncle George would be furious if the press got hold of the story. That well might happen unless she were very discreet, for the Pas coheirs were news. Also her intuition told her that she would be safer if the Conde did not suspect her true status. He was a little too interested in heiresses. As for his menacing attitude, surely he would not dare to do anything to a British citizen, however humble. Proudly she told him so.

"British citizenship is no longer the protection it once was in the days of your Empire," he told her coolly. "Nor do I intend to allow you to appeal to your Consul." He glanced around at the sunbaked countryside. "This road and this heat are not very inspiring to conversation. Will you be so good as to accompany me back to the Castillo? There you can continue to try to prove your case in cool and comfort over a long cold drink, though I warn you, I shall take a lot of convincing."

In spite of her sunglasses, the glare was making Rosalie's eyes ache, and the heat was intolerable. She blinked and swallowed, for her nose and throat were full of dust. Before her eyes swam a vision of a glass full of liquid and ice, but she said decidedly, "I refuse to go anywhere with you."

His dark eyes flickered ominously. "It would be better for you if you came willingly."

"You wouldn't dare!"

"Is that a challenge, *señorita*? If so, you are a rash woman. No one of your sex has provoked me . . . and won."

He was still holding her wrist in a purposeful grip, but his anger seemed to be abating. He was enjoying himself playing cat to her mouse, or a bird and a snake would be a more appropriate simile, she thought, for in spite of her indignation, he fascinated her. His male virility and dark good looks were making their impact upon her senses and artist's eye, piercing her perturbation. If she had had the misfortune to fall into the hands of a ruthless madman, at least he was a personable one. She had half hoped to find romance in Spain, but the men she had encountered had been disappointing. Though they were only too ready to make advances, they were short and swarthy and obviously expected her to be permissive. So she had held aloof, as she had always done where men were concerned. She had met many types in the course of her employment at Pas, but they had been uninteresting. Keen young salesmen eager to make good, more sober buyers and accountants, but any attentions they had paid her had been tainted for her by the knowledge that they were speculating how much her father would leave her.

Disillusionment had come at sixteen when she had dated a youth she had met at the recreation club to which she and Philip belonged. He was the king of the castle where the girls were concerned, and Rosalie had been flattered and pleased by his attentions, beginning to fancy herself in love. He declared he loved her and suggested becoming engaged.

Then one of his former flames enlightened her by saying, "Garth was my boyfriend until you came along, but no one has a chance with you around. Everyone knows you'll be rolling one day, and he thinks he's onto a good thing."

Her eyes opened and she began to look at Garth more critically. She discovered he was not only fickle but work-shy. It was only her prospects that had drawn him to her.

From thenceforth her relationships with boyfriends were poisoned by suspicion, and she withdrew into her painting.

Now at twenty-two she was overripe for emotional experience, and no one here knew she was an heiress, least of all this enigmatic person who was holding her. For that she should be thankful, or he might be tempted to demand a high ransom for her.

She said firmly, "You're quite wrong, you know. I'm not an adventuress, I'm only an ordinary working girl—"

His lips curled scornfully as he cut in, "But one who is anxious to improve her lot and not particular how she does it. Come, *señorita*, admit you are hoping to join that impecunious brother of yours. I suspect they have holed up somewhere until they can be married, and I may be in time to prevent that. You insist you don't know where they are, but I am sure that if you try hard you can recollect some clue to their whereabouts, and I shall do my best to assist your memory."

His grip was hurting her wrist, and his eyes were cruel. She quailed, wondering what form that assistance would take. Desperately she said, "*Señor*, you're a Spanish gentleman. Surely it's beneath your dignity to threaten a woman?"

He smiled without mirth.

"I have not threatened you . . . yet. I have merely

asked you to accept my hospitality for a little while so that we can discuss the matter. I am puzzled, you see, for it is a little hard to understand what Doña Consuelo Nuñez could find in a beggarly waiter that was preferable to a grandee of Spain."

His head went up with an arrogant gesture, and Rosalie realized how deeply his pride had been wounded. She, too, had wondered a little at Consuelo's choice, for Philip was a mere boy compared with her captor, who had the assurance and elegance of a man of the world. But he had not offered the girl his heart; he wanted only her dowry.

She said quietly, "They are young and impetuous, and they love each other very much. Love, *señor*, excuses even broken troths. You didn't love her, did you? A woman wants to be loved for herself, not her possessions." And that expressed her own feelings.

"Sentimental twaddle!" he exclaimed scornfully. "Love? Bah!" He snapped the fingers of his free hand. "It was only a flirtatious girl's fancy for a new face, and he is an adventurer after her money."

It was on the tip of her tongue to tell him that Philip would not lack for fortune in another three years, but she checked herself. Such information would entail too many explanations and would do herself no good.

"If you find them, would you want her back?" she asked, remembering she had been told he had repudiated Consuelo.

"Not I. A convent would be the right place for such soiled goods, but I want the return of the Santaella diamonds."

"But Philip couldn't afford to redeem them."

"No, damn him, but Señor Nuñez could, and would consider it a point of honor to do so, if we could discover where they are."

Rosalie sighed, for over the matter of the bracelet she was entirely in sympathy with Don Rafael. The sun beat down pitilessly on the parched landscape and his grip was paining her wrist.

"*Señor*, you're hurting me," she said wearily.

He looked curiously at her slight wrist shackled between his lean brown fingers as if he had forgotten what he held.

"Your pardon, *señorita*." He slackened his hold, but he did not release her. "Until I find him I will keep you as a pledge for the return of the heirloom."

"You can't do that, there'll be inquiries . . . ."

"Not for some time. Señor Gomez thinks you have gone home. Your loving brother believes you are still at the *parador*."

Why didn't something come by, Rosalie thought wildly—someone going to or coming from the hotel. But the countryside remained barren and empty in the heat of the early afternoon. Nothing stirred, not even a bird flew past. She was very close to the Conde's lean, muscular body, and in spite of her panic, she was becoming almost painfully aware of his masculinity.

There was a bizarre unreality about her predicament, and she could not credit that he really meant to detain her. He was only trying to scare her, and his physical attraction added piquancy to the situation.

A glint came into his eyes that caused her to suspect that he did not find her proximity distasteful and confirmed her first impression that he was susceptible to women. Some other emotion seemed to have superseded his initial wrath, for with his free hand he suddenly snatched off her sunglasses and head scarf, carelessly letting them drop onto the road; then, putting his fingers under her chin, he raised her face so that he could look into her eyes. His glance traveled over her glossy brown hair, her petal-soft cheeks, and the creamy column of her throat, and came to rest upon the full curves of her lips. A sensuous slumbrous look came into his dark eyes, a look that increased her heartbeat.

"*Muy guapa,*" he murmured, then asked abruptly. "*Su hermano,* he is like you?"

Her nerves tingling, she turned her head away from that too ardent gaze and said mechanically, "Very. We're twins."

"And twins are very close, are they not? I fancy that when he finds you are in my possession, he will agree to whatever terms I choose to dictate to ransom you."

"You're being ludicrous," she cried agitatedly, "like the villain in a stage melodrama, and you're being optimistic. As you've said, nobody will inquire for me for some time and Philip will be too . . . too occupied with his own affairs to worry."

"So we shall have some time together, and that might be . . . amusing."

"I shan't find it so!"

"*Quién sabe?*" he queried softly.

Rosalie flushed miserably. The man was crazy with jealousy and rage, and now he seemed to be finding her desirable. He thought she was a foreign girl of no account with permissive morals, and to what lengths he might go to satisfy his outrage, she shuddered to think.

Neither heard the approaching car, but as it sounded its horn, Don Rafael acted with quick resource. Enclosing her waist with his other arm, he swung her around behind his own vehicle and, bending over her, covered her face with his. Rosalie felt his thin satirical lips close over her mouth, preventing any outcry while he held her crushed against his chest.

She heard a nasal American voice from the car say with amusement, "I'm all for free expression, but they might choose somewhere more private than the middle of the road!"

A man's throaty chuckle answered it.

The car edged past Rafael's stationary vehicle and vanished in a swirl of dust.

Though she knew perfectly well the Conde's embrace had been merely to camouflage their real position and prevent her from calling out for help, Rosalie was assailed by a host of conflicting sensations engendered by that close contact. Surprise, anger and dismay mingled with a tumult in her blood. Nor did he immediately release her when the car had passed. He continued to press her body into the hardness of his, enjoying his sense of mastery over her, and his lips became bruising.

When at length he raised his head and his hold relaxed and she saw the little triumphant smile twisting his lips, sheer fury submerged all other feelings. Wrenching one arm free, she struck him across the face.

"So," he said softly, "you have claws, *bella mia*." He smiled cynically. "When a woman strikes a man's face it is an invitation, is it not, an attempt to rouse his ardor . . . or something else."

"It wasn't!" she cried stormily, struggling in his grasp. "I think you're horrible, a brute and a beast!"

Futile words, but she was bewildered by her conflicting emotions, and outraged by his behavior.

"Excellent!" Again he smiled, a thin, meaning smile that doused her fury in a trickle of fear. "You are *muy hermosa* when you are enraged, but we could find more pleasant surroundings to continue the battle, unless you wish me to embrace you every time a car passes—they will become more frequent as the day grows cooler."

"This is preposterous!" she exclaimed desperately. "And you are wasting your time, because I will never tell you my brother's whereabouts."

She felt him tense.

"So you do know where they are?"

Realizing that she had made a slip, she hastily amended, "I mean I wouldn't if I could."

"That I intend to prove. Will you please get into my car?"

"I won't!"

"Must I use force?"

"*Señor*, you wouldn't be so unchivalrous."

"Women like you are undeserving of chivalry." His mouth set grimly. "I am in earnest, *señorita*. Do not imagine that little bit of playacting just now has softened me."

The hot sun upon her uncovered nape and head, and the assault upon her emotions, began to affect Rosalie unpleasantly. The landscape wavered before her eyes, Don Rafael seemed to be retreating. As her giddiness increased, she put a hand to her eyes and swayed. Before she actually passed out, she heard the Conde utter a muttered imprecation and was aware that he picked her up in strong sinewy arms and knew no more.

When she recovered herself she found she was sitting in the front of the car, which was speeding back up the road toward the castle. The familiar ocher walls enclosing the main building undulated upward over the slope of the hill and stretched along by the road-side, marking the limits of the Conde's domain.

She murmured distressfully, "My bag, my passport!" For when last she had seen them they had been lying in the road, and without such necessary appendages she would be stranded.

"Everything of yours is in the back of the car," her companion reassured her, "including your case, sunglasses and scarf. Brute I may be, but I would not abandon your property."

He slowed down to take the right-angle turn through an open gap in the walls. The original gates had long since rusted into immobility on either side of it. Across the way was the *parador* where Rosalie could see small figures seated in the garden, the one patch of green in a desolate landscape. Only a few gnarled olive trees grew beside the Castillo de las Aguilas. Rosalie looked toward the hotel guests with yearning eyes, but they were too far away to hail.

As the car checked almost to a crawl to negotiate the narrow opening, she seized the door handle, with some idea of escaping before it was too late. Instantly he reached over and removed her groping fingers.

"I would not do that," he warned. "In your present state you would not get far. I am sorry, I did not intend to expose you to sunstroke." His lips parted in a sudden dazzling smile, the first genuine one she had seen from him, disclosing white even teeth. "You are too valuable a hostage to put at risk."

He had stopped the car while he sought to restrain her and then, his patience exhausted, he snarled, "Will you keep still, or must I knock you out?"

A glance at his face decided her to desist. He looked quite capable of carrying out his threat.

"Okay, I submit to superior force," she said weakly, then subsided into her seat, aware that her head was throbbing. The car started with a jerk, and approached the winding rutted driveway that led up to the castle's massive front door, inside which the man beside her was absolute master.

Rosalie said in a trembling voice, "If yours are an example of Spanish manners, I'm not impressed!"

To her surprise her companion colored, a dull red suffusing his olive complexion, and he muttered almost shamedly, "The circumstances excuse my actions."

"They don't, you know." She was pleased that her thrust seemed to have gone home. "You're behaving like a thug!"

He said savagely, "Then what do you call your brother's behavior? He steals my *novia* and my gift to her to pay his expenses, and you of course were to have your cut from the sale of the diamonds."

"I never dreamed of such a thing!" she cried indignantly.

"Then if you are genuinely innocent, why do you continue to cover up for them?"

"I keep telling you I had nothing to do with it."

He stopped the car in front of the entrance and turned in his seat to look at her. A faint look of puzzlement gathered about his brows as he met her candid gaze.

"It cannot be that I am mistaken about you," he said more to himself than to her, then shook his head. "No, no, you are the same as all the foreign girls who come here seeking an affair."

"A sweeping assertion. I came to work."

"At the *parador* for a pittance? I can hardly credit

that that would be an inducement to a girl with your personal assets." His eyes narrowed and glinted through half-closed lids. "The hotel was your hunting ground, and you are feigning this fine show of reluctance." Rosalie's eyes flashed and he laughed. "I am not ungenerous to those who cooperate with me, and other women have been eager to be my guests. It will be a different story when I ask you to leave."

"You flatter yourself, Don Rafael," she returned, hoping he did not mean what he seemed to be implying. "The sooner you ask me to go the more pleased I'll be."

"*Quién sabe*?" he observed imperturbably. There was something in the sensual look he bestowed upon her that caused her to blush and turn her head away. Again he looked perplexed as if this was not the reaction he was expecting.

"Come, let us go inside," he said pleasantly, but as she shrank back in her seat, he added menacingly, "If I must carry you, I warn you I won't be gentle."

"I'll walk in," she said hurriedly.

"Good, you are learning docility."

He sprang out of the car and came around to open the door for her. Rosalie slid out, very conscious of his watchful eyes.

"*Hola*, Jacobo," he shouted. "Where are you, man? We have a visitor."

He stood beside her ready to pounce if she made any movement to escape. Slowly the ponderous door opened to reveal a wizened old man, who blinked at them stupidly as his eyes met the bright sunlight.

"Bring in the lady's case and oddments," his master commanded. The old man came down the steps to the car.

"May I have my handbag?" Rosalie asked.

Don Rafael looked at her suspiciously as if expecting some trick, then laying a masterful hand on her arm, he fished in the back of the car for the desired article. Handing it to her, but retaining his hold of her, he guided her up the shallow steps. Rosalie threw a glance behind her at the hotel across the way, an oasis in the desert with its patch of greenery and gay umbrellas set out in the sun.

"You will find no refuge there," Don Rafael told her. "Señor Gomez told me he had dismissed you, and after the trouble you have caused, he would not welcome your reappearance."

So that was why Señor Gomez had urged her to hasten her departure—he knew Don Rafael was looking for her.

"Had you been to the *parador* before you intercepted me?" she asked.

"*Si*, and learned that the bird had flown, but I caught it in midflight."

With a sigh, Rosalie allowed him to lead her from the brilliant sunshine into the shadowed depths of the great hall of the Castillo de las Aguilas.

CHAPTER THREE

FROM THE OUTSIDE the Castillo de las Aguilas looked grim and forbidding, suggesting an austere discomfort. The great hall into which Rosalie stepped did nothing to dispel such expectations. Stone floored, it reached the whole height of the building to a raftered ceiling far above her head. A huge brick fireplace occupied one wall, in which stood a charcoal brazier indicating that the logs for which it was intended were difficult to procure. Narrow windows at intervals in the thick walls replaced what had once been arrow slits, and a stone staircase ascended to the upper regions. The place was scantily furnished with a few wooden benches and in one corner a suit of mail was a relic of the former garrison that had once inhabited the castle.

After the heat of the sun outside, the hall struck chill as Don Rafael closed the ponderous front door. Jacobo stood blinking in the dimness, clutching Rosalie's case, waiting for instructions.

"Take it up to the *alcoba de felicidad,*" his master commanded him. "The *señorita* will lodge there during her stay."

The happy bedroom—that sounded auspicious, Rosalie thought, but what an odd name for a chamber, unless it was a nuptial one. She darted a glance at Don Rafael and saw he was smiling enigmatically. The old man looked surprised, but he picked up her case and proceeded to toil upstairs with it.

"So you intend to keep me here?" Rosalie asked.

"For the present, yes, until you have told me all I wish to know."

She clenched her hands. "I will tell you nothing!"

He did not speak, but his face set in implacable lines. The sinister hall in which she was standing was not reassuring and she shivered in her thin suit.

"What's the use?" she went on, trying to speak reasonably in spite of her growing apprehension. Don Rafael was obviously quite mad and she was at his mercy, if he had any. "By now they will be far away where you can't reach them. I'm sorry about the diamonds, but you said perhaps the bracelet can be redeemed."

"Maybe, when I have discovered what those thieves have done with it."

"But after all, the bracelet was a gift. Señorita Nuñez may have thought she had the right to dispose of it."

"So you defend her? But her conduct is indefensible!" His eyes glinted evilly. "I will keep you until I am recompensed."

So his intention was to hold her to ransom. She wondered if Uncle George would raise it or whether he would consider that she must get out of her predicament by herself. He had warned her against just such an eventuality. As for Philip and Consuelo, she doubted very much if they would give her a thought. They would be too absorbed in each other and their own problems, and if Señor Gomez reported that she had gone, they would imagine she had departed upon some adventure of her own choosing. She reflected with satisfaction that the Conde would have no idea whom to approach for ransom money and she did not intend to enlighten him. But his next words gave her an unpleasant jolt.

"Having lost one woman I have obtained another as a substitute," he observed significantly.

A remark Rosalie found ambiguous. With difficulty she repressed a shudder. Did he mean to wreak vengeance upon her for Consuelo's infidelity, and if so, what form would it take? Her eyes traveled slowly around her forbidding surroundings. In such a place there would be dungeons, even oubliettes, chains and instruments of torture, but the Conde's implication was much less crude than physical punishment and far more humiliating.

Summoning all her resolution, for nothing would make her cringe before him, she said coolly, "I'm afraid I'm a poor substitute for the beautiful and wealthy—" she emphasized the last word, glad that her captor did not know she was coheir to the Pas empire "— Consuelo Nuñez."

Again the evil glint in his eyes. "Nevertheless you may be able to console me. I find your fair skin very appealing, and you have a spirit that would be very amusing to tame."

"What are you going to do to me?" she asked fearfully.

"That I have not yet decided," he told her. Whatever dark thoughts he was harboring, his face suddenly cleared and he continued almost affably, "My ancestral hall is not the most cheerful of reception rooms; we can do better than this, and you will be in need of that drink I promised you. Suppose we go out into the arcade? My mother is there."

Rosalie experienced a rush of relief; she had forgotten that the dowager Doña Teresa also lived at the castle. Surely Rafael could not be contemplating any excess with his mother present, and perhaps she could appeal to her for protection.

The Conde opened a door on the far side of the hall
and beckoned to her to go through it. As she did so,
she blinked in the dazzling light that met her. After the
shadowed hall it was blindingly brilliant so that for a
second she could not take in her surroundings. Then
her vision cleared and she looked about her curiously.

From stone tower to stone tower a long arcade ran
the length of the building under the floor above, sup-
ported by plain solid pillars, between which a
wrought-iron railing enclosed it. Beyond the railing
the castle walls formed a quadrangle, and directly
opposite was a whitewashed windowless wall of some
other building up which grew a vine. In the center of
the square thus formed was an ancient well, which no
longer supplied the household with water but was
used, Rosalie was to learn later, to water the cultivated
terraces that covered the hillside beyond the white
building. Against the walls on either side, several
orange trees displayed their glossy leaves and golden
fruit. The strong sunlight threw the shadows of the
railing and pillars across the floor of the arcade for
half its width; the other half was in the shade of its
roof. At first sight the place seemed deserted, wrapped
in noontide silence and heat, the black bars of the railing looking a little sinister. Then Don Rafael indicated
that she should turn to her left. She saw wicker chairs
and a small iron table set in the shaded part of the
arcade, and seated there was the dowager Condesa
Teresa de Santaella y Morena. (In Spain a married
woman places her maiden name after her husband's,
though she is never addressed by it.)

She had the same narrow high-bred face as her son,
dark eyes and hair as yet untouched with gray. She
was dressed in widow's black and an old-fashioned
black lace mantilla covered her proudly held head.

Rafael said casually, "*Madre mia,* permit me to present Señorita Smith. She will be staying with us for a while." Then he turned his attention to the jug of lemonade and tumblers on the table and liberally filled two glasses.

"Is that so?" Doña Teresa inquired.

"Felipe Smith is her brother," the Conde told her significantly, lengthening the vowel sound in Smith. "Sit down, *señorita.*" He handed Rosalie the drink. "I am afraid the ice has melted, but it is still cool."

Rosalie sipped gratefully. Don Rafael's moods seemed oddly at variance; one moment he was threatening and now he was playing the attentive host, possibly for his mother's benefit.

The Condesa's dark opaque eyes slid comprehensively over the girl's face and figure.

"Smith?" she said thoughtfully, using the same pronunciation as her son's. "There are many Smiths in England, is it not so, *señorita*?"

"It is a very common name, madam," Rosalie confirmed. "I came to Spain to work as a waitress because I wanted to see the country."

Doña Teresa seemed to be following some train of thought of her own. "Señorita Smith," she repeated. "What is your first name, *chica*?"

"Rosalie, madam."

There was a tiny pause while the Condesa's eyelids flickered.

"A pretty name," she remarked. "Too pretty for a waitress."

Rosalie glanced at her dubiously. Surely in this remote part of central Spain her name could convey nothing to her hostess? Philip Alexander had never advertised his family, and her clothes and her occupation were hardly what would be expected of an heiress.

"Our house is yours," Doña Teresa went on, using the conventional Spanish welcome to a guest, "and I hope you will enjoy your stay." Her English was as good as her son's.

Rosalie began to think that she must be dreaming. After what had gone before, the Condesa's words seemed almost farcical. She stole a quick look at Rafael's inscrutable face. He was lounging gracefully against one of the pillars of the arcade, and his mouth curled satirically. He could not have prepared his mother for her advent, since he had not known he would encounter her. He had said luck had been on his side, but Doña Teresa, whatever she thought about Rosalie's unexpected appearance, was too courteous to express any surprise. Explanations would come later, she supposed.

Surreptitiously studying Teresa de Santaella's fine face, while the woman chatted conventionally about the country and its visitors, Rosalie could not believe that she would lend herself to any dark scheme of vengeance her son might be hatching and felt reassured.

"You have been shown your room?" the Condesa asked.

"Not yet."

"Where is she lodged?" she inquired of her son.

Rafael said unconcernedly. "*La alcoba de felicidad.*"

The Condesa raised her brows. "But that is—"

"Precisely, *madre*," he interrupted her.

Doña Teresa gave Rafael an intent look and said in a low voice in her Castilian Spanish, "My son, in your frustration, do not do anything that is unworthy of you and your family."

He returned her gaze with a moody stare.

"You do not understand, this woman may appear sweet and demure, but she is a cunning schemer and deserves to be taught a lesson."

The Condesa's regard returned to Rosalie, who had not been able to follow their soft rapid speech, for her own Spanish was rudimentary and of not nearly such a pure vintage.

"It may be you are mistaken, *mi hijo.*"

"I do not think so," he returned shortly.

Doña Teresa rose to her feet.

"Come, *chica,* you will no doubt wish to freshen yourself before lunch, which has been kept back for El Conde's coming. I will show you the way." She looked back at her son and said in Spanish, "I will speak with you later when we are alone."

Rafael shrugged. "As you please, mama."

The room into which the Condesa ushered Rosalie was above the arcade and looked out upon the square below. Though the windows were grilled with the Spanish *reja,* the room in no way suggested a prison. The floor was polished wood with several fine rugs upon it, and the furnishings, though scanty, were in handsome carved wood. The bed was enormous, a fourposter covered with a blue silk spread. Adjoining the bedroom was a small tiled bathroom, evidently installed at a much later date. Before conversion it had been a powder closet.

Doña Teresa looked around the room with a loving eye.

"That was my marriage bed," she said, "and there Don Rafael was born. Alas, he was the only one."

"But, madam, am I turning you out?" Rosalie exclaimed, aghast.

"No, *chica,* I moved into a smaller room when my

husband died. This one was too full of memories. It was to have been Don Rafael's when he wed." She looked thoughtfully at Rosalie. "I do not understand why he wishes to put you in here."

Rosalie went cold as her eyes went toward the great bed, the one her host had hoped to share with Consuelo. Was this to be his subtle vengeance? But surely he could not mean to seduce her.

"Madam," she began faintly. "The Conde is an honorable man. . . ." She stopped, for she did not know if his mother had a part in what had transpired. She might condone the action he meant to take.

"Most honorable," the Condesa reassured her. "He will do you no harm, *chica*. It's a pity . . . others have not his high sense of duty." She compressed her thin lips. "But *ay de mi,* the young ones of today have not the integrity of the past."

"You're thinking of Señorita Nuñez," Rosalie suggested, "But I don't believe in arranged marriages, madam. A woman has a right to marry the man she loves even if he isn't very well off. Money can't buy happiness."

"There is not much happiness without it," Doña Teresa retorted dryly. "But evidently your brother expects to benefit from Señorita Nuñez's fortune, unless her father disinherits her."

Stung by the Condesa's contemptuous tone, Rosalie began, "Philip won't be dependent upon his wife's money . . . " and stopped as she met her hostess's interrogative eye. "He earns a good salary," she concluded lamely.

"What does he do?"

"Oh, he's in business," Rosalie said vaguely. It would never do to mention Pas.

Doña Teresa looked down her straight nose, and told her haughtily, "It is only of recent years that we of the aristocracy have admitted businessmen into our closed circle."

"But isn't Spain a republic?"

The Condesa sighed. "*Si, chica,* and many of our landed gentry have to work in offices, but they are still proud of their titles."

She looked at her watch and told Rosalie she would return shortly to bring her downstairs.

Rosalie was about to tell her not to bother, for she could find her own way, but the Condesa slipped swiftly from the room before she could intercept her, and she heard the key turn in the lock on the outside of her door.

There was something very disagreeable about the sound, and Doña Teresa's sudden exit, as if she was ashamed of what she had to do. It was a reminder of her real position, and she experienced a return of the apprehension the Spanish woman's friendliness had almost dispelled. Would she protect her from Don Rafael's vindictive temper, or was she in league with him? She had said her son would not harm her, but the locking of her door had a baleful significance.

Meanwhile a wash would be very welcome, also a change of apparel. The water was nearly cold, but it was refreshing. Delving into her case, Rosalie regretfully pushed aside the trousers and floral top she normally would have worn. Such garb would only increase Don Rafael's poor opinion of her character.

She had several plain nylon dresses, which did not take up much room in her case, and though they were sleeveless, she hoped their plainness would not offend Spanish sensibilities. She noticed her wrist was becoming discolored where the Conde had gripped it. That was hardly surprising, for the man was a brute. Yet even as she came to that conclusion, her stomach churned in retrospect as she remembered his bruising kisses. Her northern frigidity had been stirred by his soft sensuous voice, the gleam in his black eyes, the hint of smoldering fires.

She looked at herself in the long mirror in the bedroom, comparing herself with Consuelo Nuñez, and could find little to recommend her. She had good skin, the famous English complexion of peaches and cream, her eyes were large and expressive, but there it ended. She had none of the Peruvian girl's sexiness, her feminine curves and lustrous hair and eyes. Her slight form looked childish and virginal, nothing there to rouse a lusty Spanish male. But he had said she was beautiful when she was angry. . . . She should not have slapped his face; it had been a useless provocative protest and would give him an excuse to inflict some further indignity.

A knock on the door recalled her from her musings and she heard the key turn.

"Come in," she called, and her heart leaped as Rafael entered the room.

He, too, had bathed and changed, and was wearing a cream-colored suit, the jacket open to display a scarlet cummerbund that gave a barbaric touch of his appearance; she almost expected to see earrings in his ears.

"You!" she exclaimed nervously. "What do you want?"

"Only a few words with you before we join the Condesa." His glance slid over her appraisingly. "You look charming."

"I don't want any compliments," she said stormily, aware that her pulses had quickened under his slumbrous gaze and furious with herself for her reaction. "Seeing as I'm held in duress, they're a little out of place."

"Are they ever out of place? May I not show my appreciation of my captive's charms?" He was smiling wickedly.

"So long as you confine yourself to words . . . " she began, then blushed hotly, realizing her speech was ill-chosen. "Well, what did you want to say?" she concluded briskly, wishing he would not stare at her so fixedly.

"Merely to ask you to give me your parole. It would make life much more pleasant for all concerned."

"Meaning that if I promise not to try to escape, I won't be locked up?"

"Crudely put, but that is the idea. If you give me your promise, we can treat you like a guest—an honored guest."

Her chin went up. "And if I won't?"

His eyes narrowed. "I would hate to have to put you in chains."

Involuntarily she quailed. "Surely even you couldn't be such a barbarian."

"I never threaten what I am not prepared to perform," he told her. "But please do not try to provoke me. Won't you give me your promise?"

"Seeing that you have such a low opinion of me, you can't expect me to keep it."

He gave her a long penetrating look, which Rosalie met without flinching, noticing how long his eyelashes were. They gave a deceptive look of softness to his beautiful eyes.

"That is a risk I am prepared to take," he told her. "You will hand over your passport and your money, naturally, as an extra precaution." He smiled, a swift charming smile that illuminated his normally stern face. "Unlike Consuelo you are English, and on the continent we always used to say, 'Word of an Englishman,' meaning a promise would be kept. You would not wish to let your countrymen down, *señorita*?"

Diverted by the mention of Consuelo, she asked, "Did Señorita Nuñez make you any promises, or did her father make them on her behalf?"

He seemed to be considering, and then he sighed.

"Perhaps you are right. It was her father who arranged the betrothal. I did not have much contact with the lady herself. It is not considered correct in this country, you know."

"That's what's so wrong," Rosalie declared emphatically. "How can you get to know each other, decide if you're suited until too late?"

He drew himself up haughtily and said coldly, "A man does not take liberties with a woman he respects. I would not wish to get to know, as you put it, the woman I meant to wed before marriage."

He had misconstrued her words, but whether deliberately or not she was uncertain. One thing was obvious: he did not respect her, Rosalie.

"But in England I know it is different," he went on, "and very different in other northern countries. *Por Dios*, the Swedish beauties who throng our beaches in the summertime have first bewildered and then corrupted our young men." His eyes kindled at some sensual memory. "They are *muy hermosa*, but we would never marry them."

Rosalie suspected that he had not scrupled to avail himself of the favors offered to him by the girls he despised.

"But I'm not like that," she said firmly.

"That time will show," he returned imperturbably. "Come, *señorita*, no more evasion. Give me your promise."

She hesitated, for she would have to keep her word if she did so.

"Surely you would prefer to come and go as you please?" he said persuasively, and his eyes went to the ponderous lock on the door.

"But how long do you intend to keep me here?" she inquired.

"That depends upon your cooperation."

"Do you still imagine I can give you any information about my brother's whereabouts?"

"I think if you will condescend to discuss the situation frankly and tell me something of your history, I might gain a clue, or I might be persuaded to let the matter rest."

Rosalie's eyes became wary. What new development was this? Why did he wish to probe into her antecedents? Her life was an open book, except for the fact she did not want to disclose to this seemingly rapacious Spaniard her connection with Pas. Since he had been defrauded of Consuelo's dowry, he might seek to recompense himself by cashing in upon her own expectations. She smiled wryly, picturing Uncle George's dismay if Don Rafael demanded a huge ransom. He would have to pay it to release her, and that would serve him right for his strict interpretation of her father's will.

Don Rafael was watching the expressions flitting

across her face and was right in concluding that she had something to hide, though her secret was not what he thought it was.

"Be that as it may," he said pleasantly, "I am still waiting for your promise, and I am sure you must be hungry, as I am."

She decided she had nothing to gain by refusing, and as he had said, existence would be much more pleasant if she were not kept under lock and key.

"Very well, I promise," she agreed, "and I do keep my word, *señor*."

"Excellent, and now, please be so good as to hand over your passport and any cash you may have on you."

In resentful silence, she opened her bag and extracted her passport and the wad of money Señor Gomez had given her.

"That represents my return fare," she said reproachfully as she handed the bills to him.

"I thought you might have that," he said meaningly. He meticulously counted the money, and made a note of the amount in his wallet. "This will be returned to you in due course." He slipped money and documents into his jacket pocket. "Even if you are tempted to break your word, I do not think you would get far penniless and without papers. And now, shall we go and eat?"

He pushed the half-closed door open for her and stood aside to let her pass. Rosalie stalked by him with her head in the air and bitter resentment in her heart.

The meal was served not in the great hall but in a room to one side, which looked out onto the quadrangle. It was furnished with shabby grandeur, a long polished table, carved chairs and sideboard, with somewhat moth-eaten tapestry upon its bare walls.

It was a simple meal, cold chicken and smoked ham, tomatoes, homemade bread, goat's cheese and grapes, food that was all produced locally. Since the water was not fit for drinking, Rosalie accepted the manzanilla that was offered to her.

"It came from the south," the Condesa told her. "It is the wine of Sevilla where we have connections."

Rosalie began to lose all sense of reality. Her host and hostess chatted pleasantly to her as if she were in truth a guest, but she was not here by her own will, and she was aware of the surreptitious scrutiny of two pairs of night-dark eyes. The Condesa's were frankly curious, but Don Rafael's were completely unrevealing. Occasionally his lips curled as if he were enjoying some secret joke. Rosalie was relieved that he no longer seemed menacing, but she could not imagine what he hoped to gain by keeping her there. She was still more relieved when at the conclusion of the meal he said he had business to attend to in connection with the farm and regretted he must leave them. The Condesa conducted Rosalie back to the chairs in the arcade, and Jacobo brought them coffee.

"Where is the farm?" Rosalie asked, when he had left them.

Doña Teresa indicated the vine-draped wall in front of them.

"That is the back of the farmhouse. On the other side the hillside is terraced. We grow all our own fruit and vegetables, and we also keep goats, poultry and pigs, so we are practically self-supporting. The estate extends over several hectares and includes some olive groves, but it has shrunk from what it once was and we can no longer keep horses, which used to be my husband's pride." She sighed. "I do not know how much longer we can maintain the castle . . . now."

Rosalie knew she was thinking of Consuelo's lost fortune and felt a spurt of antagonism. Neither she nor her son had any thought for the girl's happiness. All they wanted was her money.

The Condesa went on to tell her that the Santaellas possessed a small property in the much more productive region of Andalusia, the income from which paid the taxes on Las Aguilas.

"Castile and Aragon are the land of the black legend," she informed her. "They are sunstruck, stark and menacing, cruel country with a cruel history, but Andalusia is that of the white legend—white buildings, red soil, lush plains, laughter and song. Maybe we will retire there if Don Rafael has to sell the castle, but he so dislikes the idea of it becoming another *parador*, and nobody wants it for anything else. It is offensive to our pride to allow our ancestral home, and it has been ours for centuries, to be so degraded." She evidently identified herself entirely with her husband's people.

Privately Rosalie thought that such pride was an expensive luxury. The Castillo obviously needed extensive repairs and modernizing to be comfortable. Nor could life in it be very amusing for the Condesa, for she was unable to drive the car, their one extravagance, and she did not entertain. It was unlikely since Consuelo had eluded him that Don Rafael would be able to capture another heiress.

Later, when the sun was sinking and a faint breeze produced some air, her hostess suggested that Rosalie might like to tour the house, and she accepted with alacrity. From one of the towers she was able to look out over the roof of the farmhouse, and she saw that the land on the far side of the castle was much less bleak and barren than the land she was familiar with.

There were patches of cultivation on the descending terraces as the Condesa had said, fruit and vegetables, but she was informed they had to be watered morning and evening to survive.

"Jacobo and his grandson do that," she explained. "The Lorcas live in the farmhouse, and Dolores, his son's wife, does our cooking. Come and be introduced to them."

They descended to the vaultlike kitchen where the vast range was augmented by a humble oil stove. Strings of onions and garlic hung from the soot-blackened rafters, and an ancient crone, who turned out to be Jacobo's wife, was turning the handle of a small churn, making goat's cream into butter. The Lorca family comprised the old couple, Dolores and her husband and their two sons, boys of eight and ten.

"In Spain the *abuelos* and *abuelas* live with their families, and they still have their uses," Doña Teresa remarked, watching the old woman's efforts. "We do not put them in ghettos like you do in your country."

"We don't do that," Rosalie protested.

"What else are your old people's homes? Here the young and old live happily together without being segregated. They are all part of the family."

Rosalie thought it would be too difficult to explain the economic stresses that led to the isolation of old people, the principal one being lack of accommodation. Of that there seemed to be plenty in the castle and the farm.

"It isn't always practical to be all together," she said, wondering what she and Philip would have done with two sets of grandparents on their hands. Actually they had none living.

"The English are a coldhearted people," the Condesa said loftily, as she led the way back to the arcade.

Rafael did not reappear and the Condesa had their evening meal brought out to them on a tray. A lantern was lit above their heads and big moths and other insects circled around it. Jacobo squirted insecticide into the shadows to discourage mosquitoes and gnats. Fireflies gleamed among the foliage of the orange trees, and cicadas kept up a lively chorus. Finally when a bat skimmed over the Condesa's head, she suggested it was time to go indoors. They repaired to a room on the opposite side to the dining room, which Doña Teresa called the *sala*, and here she produced a vast workbox. It seemed that she occupied most of her time doing needlework. She turned and patched her own clothes and Don Rafael's, and embroided squares to cover the worn places on the furniture. Rosalie was no needlewoman, but she admitted that she sketched in her leisure hours. Forthwith her hostess demanded to see her work and she fetched her portfolio. Doña Teresa was much amused by her impressions of the guests at the *parador*.

"You have much talent," she told her, "surprising in a *criada*, but then you are not really a maidservant, are you? I am told foreign students often hire themselves out to hotels during their holidays, but don't your relatives mind?"

"Mine couldn't care less," Rosalie told her, "and at home I'm employed in a shop."

Her hostess gave her a shrewd glance.

"Is that so?" she murmured, and Rosalie sensed that she did not believe her. "I would be honored," she went on, "if you would make a picture of me."

Rosalie had been itching to do so ever since she had met her. The Condesa's proud profile framed by her lace mantilla was shouting to be portrayed. Her features were very like the masculine ones that had so intrigued her, but she would never dare to ask Don Rafael to pose for her. However, there was nothing to stop her from drawing him from memory so long as he never saw the fruit of her pencil.

Time crept by while Rosalie drew and Condesa sewed. As the minutes passed, Rosalie became more and more nervous, her ears stretched for the sounds of Don Rafael's return. She was expecting the inquisition to which he had promised to subject her, and she felt too weary to be able to cope with him. Spaniards always kept late hours, and he would think nothing of starting to question her in the small hours of the morning. Some time after midnight Doña Teresa remarked, to Rosalie's relief, that he did not appear to be coming and it was time they both went to bed.

"I am glad that he has found a diversion to take his mind off his troubles," she said as she folded away her sewing.

Rosalie wondered what form that diversion had taken; there did not seem to be much in the surrounding area except the *parador*, and he would not want to go there now. Her hostess apologized for his nonappearance, saying it was unlike him to neglect a guest. Under the circumstances Rosalie was only too glad to be neglected, but she said politely that of course it did not matter and meekly followed Doña Teresa up the stone stairs.

Although she was very tired she could not relax. Uneasily she paced her bedroom, wondering if she dared undress. The great bed seemed to dominate the room, the marriage bed of the Santaellas. She could not rid herself of the feeling that Don Rafael meant to take his revenge in an only too obvious manner. He had said that having lost one woman he had found another to console him. Though Doña Teresa had hinted he was finding solace elsewhere tonight and did not seem to think he was harboring any evil intentions toward herself, she had been surprised when Rafael had told her where he had lodged the guest. Rosalie's fears had been lulled during the uneventful evening, but now they returned to her in full flood. True, the Condesa had told him she would speak to him alone, and possibly she had reasoned him out of his madness, but Rosalie judged her to be a devious and subtle woman, who might say one thing while she meant another, and she might well be as incensed against her as her son was.

Strung to a high pitch of expectancy as she was, Rosalie's eyes continually turned toward the iron-studded door, wondering what she would do if it began to open. The thick walls excluded all sound, and the entrance to the castle was on the opposite side, so she could not tell if Don Rafael had returned.

A thought struck her. Going to the door and opening it cautiously, she sought the key on the other side. Extricating it from the lock, she froze as she heard soft footfalls along the passage leading to it. Shutting it hastily, she locked it on her side and stood listening, tense in every nerve, expecting an imperious knock. Nothing happened.

Then at last she undressed and sank wearily into the capacious bed, falling at once into deep sleep. But before she became unconscious she was aware of a vague sense of anticlimax, and her dreams were haunted by a dark narrow face with a charming smile.

CHAPTER FOUR

THE INQUISITION Rosalie had so dreaded never did take place. Don Rafael's manner toward her changed completely. No longer aggressive, always a little aloof, he treated her with a distant courtesy, but both he and his mother were continually watching her. At first she thought they were expecting her to try to escape, but as time went by she began to suspect that if she walked out of the castle, no one would try to stop her. She could not do so until she was released from her promise and her passport and money were returned, and she was reluctant to raise the subject until her host did in case she precipitated some kind of crisis. She surmised that if truth were told, Rafael de Santaella was a little at a loss to know what to do with her.

Having, in the heat of his rage and chagrin, yielded to a vengeful impulse, he had secured her, as she was the nearest he could get to the delinquents, with some vague idea of making her pay for the affront her brother had put upon him. Now that his temper had cooled he no longer harbored any such desire, nor did he even wish to question her, for it was obvious that Philip and Consuelo were by now beyond his reach, and that they would be married as soon as possible. He contented himself by making some sneering remarks about premarital precipitancy, rousing Rosalie hotly in their defense. Though the couple were deeply in love, she knew they would wait for their union to be legalized before they consummated it.

"Philip will respect Señorita Nuñez's upbringing," she said firmly. "I tell you he loves her and would not do anything to distress her."

"You think so much of this love?" Rafael asked sardonically. "You believe that it justifies everything?"

When he put his question, the three of them were sitting in the arcade, watching the sunset flush the sky. Don Rafael had been out all day and on his return had changed into his white coat and black sash. With Doña Teresa's somber draperies, their dark hair and eyes, they created a symphony in black and white. Rosalie's rose-colored dress was the only touch of color in the group. Jacobo had brought out glasses and a jug of Sangria, a mixture of red wine, mineral water and fruit juices. They were enjoying an aperitif before their evening meal.

In answer to Rafael's inquiry, Roaalie said, "not everything, but it isn't as if there was any real barrier between them."

"Only a broken troth," he observed moodily.

"And a diamond bracelet." She raised her clear candid eyes to his. "Be honest, Don Rafael, you didn't care a fig for Señorita Nuñez as a person; it's only the bracelet and her dowry that you regret. You were completely indifferent to her."

She waited a little anxiously for his response, for it was a daring thing to have said. But it was Consuelo's justification.

He stared into the gray depths of her eyes with a considering expression, as if he were assessing her. Rosalie wished she could read his thoughts. Did he still believe she was a cheap go-getter? She was hoping he had revised his opinion of her now he had been in daily contact with her.

"You are still young enough to cherish romantic illusions," he said at length. "A good marriage requires a more stable foundation than a sudden infatuation. It requires similar backgrounds, and of course nationality. Consuelo would not have found me neglectful as a husband." His eyes gleamed as he recalled the girl's beauty. "But I am a practical man and not one to be misled by the lure of the senses. I needed that money to preserve Las Aguilas, but that is no great matter." Doña Teresa made a movement of surprise. "The bracelet, however, is something else. Its loss I will never cease to regret. It has been worn by all the Santaella brides. You did not wish to give it up, did you, mama?"

"I only valued it because your father placed it on my wrist, and I never wore it after I was married, because it was too heavy," Doña Teresa told them. "What I do regret is that it will not be available for the woman you do marry, *mi hijo.*"

Rafael shrugged. "I shall never marry now."

"Of course you will," his mother told him briskly. "In fact you must, for you are the last of your line."

"Then I will marry a *campesina*. At least she would appreciate the honor," he said bitterly.

They seemed to have forgotten Rosalie's presence, and she sat back in the shadows watching the two fine faces. Rafael's fierce pride was rejecting the idea of wooing another woman, but Doña Teresa was determined that he should do so to preserve his heritage and his family name.

"Peasants have no money," she pointed out. "It is your duty to marry money, and there are other heiresses beside Consuelo."

"Then find me one," he said savagely.

"Perhaps she is not very far to seek," she said significantly.

"I know who you have in mind, but I am not persuaded she is suitable," he returned.

The Condesa nodded her head with a sphinxlike smile.

"She will be, when she has been taught to conform."

Of the two, Rosalie thought, the Condesa was almost the most formidable, and she pitied the poor girl she had selected to be instructed in conformity. She knew that the family name and possessions meant a great deal to her hostess, and she could understand why she shrank from seeing the commercialization of her ancestral home—the Morenas were cousins of the Santaellas and so she regarded it as such. The civil war had nearly ruined both families, and Doña Teresa was ruthless in her efforts to reinstate them. But she had no right to sacrifice her son's happiness to bricks and stones, though as far as Rosalie knew, Rafael's heart had never been involved and presumably he would accept the next moneyed girl as indifferently as he had accepted Consuelo. She wondered whom Doña Teresa had found and felt sickened by the cold-bloodedness of her planning, though it was nothing to her whom Rafael married. He did not deserve a loving wife, for he had shown himself lacking in consideration and he had acted in a tyrannical and threatening manner toward herself. She hoped the girl would be able to stand up for herself, otherwise she would soon be flattened—but wasn't that what was expected of a Spanish wife?

She had to admit that Don Rafael no longer showed any sign of tyranny or threats since she had given her parole. He set himself to play the courteous host and made no restrictions, though he did not suggest she go outside the castle grounds. Not that she had any wish to do so, for there was only the rather dull village and the *parador* within miles of them. Over their leisurely meals he told her a great deal about the country and its customs, as well as some of his family history, which went back to Ferdinand and Isabella and the Christian knights who had fought to drive out the Moors.

"Actually the Moriscos brought us a much finer civilization than existed anywhere else in Europe at that time," he told her. "And they were less cruel than their Christian opponents. There are fine examples of their buildings still remaining in the south. You have heard of the Alhambra, of course? They were a very clean people and always taking baths. The medieval knights existed in dirt and squalor."

Though he never questioned her, as he had threatened to do, he pounced upon every item she let slip about her life. Thus he learned that she had served at a cashier's desk, but instead of sneering as she had expected, he gave her a long speculative look she could not interpret.

So a week passed, and then one afternoon when the Condesa was taking a siesta and Rosalie was sitting a little disconsolately in the arcade trying to read a Spanish book, a letter came from Philip. Don Rafael brought it to her and she looked up in surprise at his approach, for he usually avoided being alone with her, considering such a situation not correct. Then she saw the envelope in his hand.

"For you, Señorita Smith."

Taking it she recognized the handwriting and saw it was addressed to the *parador*.

"But does Señor Gomez know I'm here?"

"*Claro*, obviously."

She flushed. Of course, everyone must know that she was at Las Anguilas. Dolores Lorca gossiped with Juana. She wondered what they all made of it.

"Are you not anxious to read your epistle?"

She would have much preferred to peruse it in private, but since he was obviously waiting to hear the news, she had no option but to open it. She did not want to provoke him into taking it from her.

Philip was as she had expected staying with their mother and was shortly to be married to Consuelo. He asked if "old Gomez" would give her a couple of days off to attend the wedding, but pointed out that it would be a big expense for her. He was sorry he could not offer to help her. He could hardly ask his bride to oblige, and though satisfactory negotiations with Uncle George were pending they had not yet materialized. Ma Pas, which was his disrespectful name for Mrs. Smith, would let her have a bed for the night following the reception, but she didn't like demands made upon her hospitality. "She's lazy and doesn't like putting herself out even for her family," he commented, which was no news to Rosalie. In a postscript he added, "We're deliriously happy." It was a perfunctory invitation and obviously it had never crossed Philip's mind that he might have made trouble for his sister.

Rosalie folded the thin paper and looked up to meet Rafael's questioning gaze. He was seated on the iron railing, his back against a pillar, swinging one foot, his hands thrust into his pants pockets.

"It is from the twin brother?" he asked with assumed, at least she supposed it was assumed, carelessness.

She nodded. "It's an invitation to his wedding."

"Oh. Will you go?"

"How can I?"

"Would you if you could?"

She hesitated. Consuelo's advent had loosened the ties between her and her brother. He was absorbed in his love, which was only right, but he had become remote. "I don't know," she said finally.

It had not been suggested she should be a bridesmaid, nor could she have afforded a dress if it had. Paris would be very expensive and nobody seemed particularly anxious to welcome her. She wondered fleetingly what Philip meant by satisfactory negotiations pending. Was Uncle George about to relent and allow him to borrow from the trust? A tide of resentment welled up in her. Everything seemed to be going Philip's way, and neither her mother nor her uncle had spared a thought for her, presumably toiling away at the *parador*, except for the offer of a bed for one night.

"Where are they?" The abrupt question startled her out of her brooding and recalled the man who was the prime loser in this alliance.

"In Paris," she told him frankly.

"So they are out of reach. No chance of a dramatic intervention." He smiled wryly. "Has Señor Nuñez disinherited his daughter?"

"Philip doesn't mention him."

"How strange, that I should have thought would have been a matter of supreme importance to him. He cannot keep Consuelo Nuñez on a waiter's wages."

"Philip has, er, got a better job."

"It will need to be a good one." He leaned against the pillar behind him and regarded her through halfshut lids. "But no doubt they are still subsisting upon the proceeds from the bracelet. It was very valuable."

Rosalie said nothing; she was resolving that she would make Philip tell her to whom he had sold it. If there was any chance of redeeming it, she must prevail upon Uncle George to buy it back and return it to the Don. Its acquisition was dishonest, and that no Smith would condone. She had great hopes she could persuade him to see it her way.

Rafael looked at her downcast face. "Sure you are not longing to join in the celebrations?" he gibed. "No pangs of conscience need disturb your pleasure."

"Actually they would," she said quietly. "I was wondering if the bracelet could be recovered."

"You know I have not the means to do so, and now I have lost touch with Señor Nuñez, who seems to have accepted its sale with equanimity."

She flashed him a quick look, but said nothing. That was not what she had in mind.

"So it is goodbye to the Santaella diamonds," he observed regretfully.

"You might be able to buy them back when you marry the rich bride your mother has selected for you," she suggested.

"Why, so I could," he agreed, a little enigmatic smile edging his lips. "But would you consider it ethical to purchase my love token with my *esposa*'s own money?"

"It would be as ethical as giving a love token when love didn't come into it," she told him sharply.

"What a feminine viewpoint! But you are jumping to conclusions. Love might come into it. I am not incapable of tender emotion, though you seem to doubt it."

Rosalie caught the satirical gleam in his eyes and turned her head away. Tenderness seemed unlikely in connection with him, but she had no means of assessing what capabilities did lie beneath his arrogant exterior. The thought of his affections being bestowed upon some young woman was oddly unwelcome to her.

"I hope for both your sakes you do fall in love with her," she told him.

"How kind of you, but my feelings are the least of the problem." He looked away across the quadrangle to the clustering grapes on the distant wall. "I, er, have been told she is a foreigner."

His words gave Rosalie a jolt. From a nebulous abstraction his new *novia* began to take shape. The Condesa really had found a suitable partner for him.

"Does that matter?" she asked. "Señorita Nuñez was a Peruvian."

"Exactly, and you know what happened, although she was of Spanish extraction and she should have known how to behave."

"Been more submissive, you mean," Rosalie told him tartly. "But I see your point; most foreigners aren't submissive. It depends what nationality she is and whether she wants to live in Spain."

She looked at him questioningly, but he said nothing, meditatively stroking one sideburn with a long forefinger. His fine profile was etched against the golden light flooding the courtyard, and her eyes dwelt upon it wistfully. Enigmatic creature she thought, for at that moment he was as cool and impassive as a figure carved in stone, but she knew how he could flash into sudden passion. If ever he did love he would be devastating, and although outwardly paying lip service to a strict convention, he would break all the rules if the incentive were strong enough. He would be a problem for any Nordic woman, if he chose so unwisely.

"I hope she is a Latin," she remarked, following her train of thought.

"Why?"

"Because—please don't think me impertinent—but then she would understand your way of life and, er, your temperament. Besides, you seem inclined to think that foreign freedoms spell wantonness. They don't, you know."

"I will admit I find them difficult to condone."

"Well, there you are!" she exclaimed triumphantly.

He turned his head from the contemplation of the grapes and looked at her thoughtfully. In spite of the heat, Rosalie contrived to look as fresh as an English spring morning. The thin green dress she was wearing emphasized the clarity of her complexion—she had to rinse out her garments every night to keep them immaculate and the thin nylon was drip-dried by the next day. Her hair shone with a copper sheen, while her gray eyes were earnest, as if she found this question of Don Rafael's bride a matter of the gravest concern. Actually, she did. He had been let down once, and she almost passionately hoped he would be luckier the second time, though to her way of thinking the auguries were not good.

"You would only marry an Englishman?"

The unexpected question disconcerted her. She dropped her eyes and fingered Philip's letter nervously.

"I don't think I shall ever marry," she returned. "When the time comes I intend to dedicate myself to painting." Flurried by the abrupt change to her own prospects, she'd spoken incautiously.

"When the time comes? What time? What do you mean?"

Instantly she was on guard.

"Oh, I'm sure an opportunity will occur," she told him vaguely.

"Perhaps you hope that when your brother gets his hands on the Nuñez fortune he will help you?"

About to say that nothing would induce her to touch a penny of it, she checked herself. For a second she had an impulse to confide in him, tell him about her expectations, that when she was twenty-five she could do exactly as she pleased . . . but a certain avidness in his dark regard restrained her. He might imagine she was seeking to enhance herself in his eyes, since he thought so much of money.

"Perhaps," she agreed.

He looked away again.

"You will find a paintbrush a cold bedfellow," he observed satirically.

"At least it won't be mercenary," she retorted, and saw him wince. "But we were discussing your matrimonial prospects, not mine," she concluded brightly.

"My bride has not yet materialized."

"Oh? Indeed? I thought from the way you were talking it was all settled, or nearly so."

"Eventually it may be—if all goes well."

"Perhaps the lady is hesitating?"

He looked faintly embarrassed. "The Condesa is sure she will yield when the proposition is put to her."

"I hope Doña Teresa won't try to put pressure on her," Rosalie said, thinking that his mother would be relentless to attain her ends, and she appeared to be doing the negotiating.

"That may not be necessary. Some women have, er,

found me most presentable," Don Rafael told her haughtily.

I'm sure they have, Rosalie thought drearily, *and I'm one of them.* The idea of Rafael using his personal assets to charm a wealthy woman was repugnant to her. He had not appealed to Consuelo—she had been afraid of him—but Rosalie thought she was probably an exception, so much so that her rejection had been incomprehensible to Don Rafael, wounding his vanity and rousing the devil in him.

"I think before you start to court her, it would be better—wiser—to let me go," she said dully.

He turned toward her again.

"So you are really set upon leaving us?" he asked.

Rosalie pleated her skirt with nervous fingers, suddenly aware that she did not want to leave the Castillo at all. Little by little, Don Rafael had come to dominate her thoughts and fill her imagination. Her portfolio contained a variety of sketches of him: Rafael in a ruff and steel helmet—the *conquistador*; in a velvet cloak and doublet—the grandee; even one in a Moorish robe, the Caliph of Granada. They had been the outcomes of idle fancy, and she had not yet faced their implication and the utter folly of allowing her thoughts to dwell with such concentration upon him.

Dimly aware that she must protect herself from that too penetrating gaze, she said sharply, "You forget I'm bound by my promise, and my wishes have never been consulted."

"And if I release you from your parole you will immediately depart for Paris?"

"I think it is more than time I left," she told him, feeling she would be wise to avoid any further involvement.

"You do, do you?" His face darkened. He swung himself off his perch on the rail and, standing before her, said harshly, "It is as I supposed—Spain has no appeal for you. You are weary of this primitive place and yearning for the bright lights, the big stores and the company of young people as foolish as yourself." He was lashing himself to greater fury, though for what reason she could not imagine, unless it was the thought of Consuelo's wedding, as his next words suggested. "You want to prance up the aisle in the wake of that perfidious woman who was to have been *my* bride. No doubt that would give you infinite satisfaction. You would consider it retribution for the way I treated you at the time of our encounter in the road. You give me no credit for having tried to make amends. You, a mere *criada*, have been received here like the noblest lady in the land."

Rosalie tried to interrupt, but he swept on regardless, his voice deepening in intensity, his eyes flashing.

"So, you shall have your way. Go. I will not detain you longer. Get up and go. Did you hear me?" She had not moved. "*Váyase,* pack up your things. Get out at once!"

He turned his back upon her as if the sight of her offended him, and clutched the top of the railing so hard that his knuckles showed white through the brown skin.

Rosalie was overwhelmed by this sudden attack. She stared blankly at the Conde's taut back. Unpredictable creature—he had brought her to Las Aguilas by force and now was evicting her with equal violence. But she could not depart there and then without preparing for her journey, and he must have forgotten that he still held her passport and money. A surge of anger washed over her. His arrogance was abominable! Then it occurred to her that she had a means of retaliation he had overlooked.

"I'm certainly not going to lug my case down to the village at this time of day," she said firmly, remaining anchored in her chair. "It was bad enough last time and the weather's hotter now. Besides, I must make some reservations and say goodbye to the Condesa, and you've still got my passport and money. If you want to get rid of me you must do so in a more considerate manner, and I think I've a right to ask for some compensation, that is, unless you want me to go to the police and tell them that you abducted me."

He swung around to face her.

"You would do that?"

"Certainly I will if you won't play ball. I don't suppose even the Conde de las Aguilas is above the law, and this is a civilized country, isn't it?"

"You might find yourself involved in considerable unpleasantness," he warned.

"And so might you."

He looked at her uncertainly. "You would have to *prove* you had been detained against your will, which of course I would deny," he said haughtily. His lip curled sardonically. "Women usually come willingly to my house. You would also revive all the scandal about the elopement."

Rosalie sighed, her anger abating. She had no intention of going to the police, she merely resented her summary eviction.

"Well, if you'll be more reasonable, perhaps I won't," she conceded.

He stared at her for some moments in silence, while tension built up between them. She sensed his stubborn pride was battling with his better feelings. She remained seated in her chair, one leg negligently crossed over the other, assuming a nonchalance she was far from feeling. Suddenly he relaxed.

"Forgive me," he said apologetically. "I spoke without thought. Of course, I did not mean that you must rush away without due preparation."

"It sounded like it," she pointed out.

He smiled faintly. "I was nettled to learn you found my hospitality so irksome."

"Is hospitality the right word?"

"Do you prefer imprisonment?" he demanded with a flash of anger. He checked himself. "But I will recompense you. A cash settlement, you understand, is difficult for me, but do you really want to go to this wedding? You seemed a little reluctant."

"I am. I won't go."

"No?"

Rosalie turned her head away. No need to tell him that she felt she would be unwelcome, with Philip absorbed in nuptial bliss, and her mother begrudging her a room in the house. Besides, her sympathies inclined toward Don Rafael. He had been treated very badly.

"No," she said firmly.

"Then are you in any great hurry to return to your own country?"

"I had intended to spend the rest of the summer in Spain."

He sat down in the chair opposite to her, all trace of his former passion dissipated.

"At the *parador*?" he asked.

"I had no alternative."

"Ah, but perhaps I can offer one." She looked at him in surprise.

"The Condesa and I are going to the Casa Blanca," he told her. "That is the name of my house in Andalusia. It occurred to us that you might like to come with us—you said you wanted to see the south."

"You want to keep tabs on me?" she suggested doubtfully, for she could think of no other reason for the invitation.

"Certainly not." He hesitated, looking at his fingernails, while Rosalie watched him eagerly; she had long wanted to visit the south, but could he be going to make any proposition that would be acceptable to her?

Rafael seemed to come to a decision. His manner became impersonal and businesslike as he faced her across the small table between them.

"It is like this, Señorita Smith. I shall be very occupied when we reach Cordoba province and the Condesa will be lonely. She needs a companion. She likes you, and in fact it is her suggestion. We are offering you employment in that capacity, and in addition to your expenses, we will pay you pocket money." He smiled ruefully. "We can run to that. It would be a more congenial occupation for you than that of waitress at a hotel, would it not?"

"It would indeed," Rosalie exclaimed.

"Then can we take it as settled?"

It was Rosalie's turn to hesitate. She knew it would be wiser to break her association with the Santaellas if she wished to preserve her peace of mind, but the prospect was alluring; the long journey back to Pas was not.

"We wish to start the day after tomorrow, so I am afraid I must ask for your answer now," Don Rafael went on. "If you are not coming, we must dispose of you before we can leave and it will take me a little time to make the necessary arrangements for you." He smiled mischievously. "Since I do not want you to bring the police here to arrest me."

"I . . . I didn't really mean that," Rosalie faltered. She looked searchingly into his dark, narrow face, which was so unrevealing, and added impulsively, "Do you want me to come?"

He turned his head away as if unwilling to meet her candid gaze and shrugged.

"I? It is immaterial to me what you decide to do. As I said, it is the Condesa who desires your company. She considers it would be a satisfactory arrangement if you are agreeable."

Rosalie was disappointed; it would have been so much more pleasing to her ego if he had declared he was anxious for her presence . . . but much more dangerous.

"Thank you, I . . . I'd like to come and I'll do my best to entertain the Condesa," she told him. "It's very kind of you to suggest it."

His eyebrows shot up. "Kind? It is you who will be doing us a favor. But you are perfectly free to go to Paris if you would prefer to do so and I will give you every assistance to facilitate your journey." He paused and shot her a sideways glance. "It might be wiser for you to do so."

"How so?" she asked anxiously.

"Oh, Andalusia is very hot at this time of year," he told her evasively.

His lack of enthusiasm increased her own.

"As if I cared about that!" she cried recklessly. "I want to see Andalusia badly, and this is a heaven-sent opportunity."

He smiled wryly, but whether at her eagerness or his own thoughts she did not know.

"*Sí, niña,* and only a fool misses his opportunities. *Bien,* I have warned you, so on your head be it."

Rosalie felt a little stab of uneasiness at this ambiguous remark, but surely he could only be referring to the weather. Her misgivings were entirely dispelled when the Condesa thanked her warmly for agreeing to come with her.

"You will not find me exigent," she told her. "It is someone to talk to I desire, and we are *compatible,* are we not? It seems an ideal arrangement since your holiday time is not over yet."

Doña Teresa persisted in believing that Rosalie was a student filling in her long vacation with a working holiday in Spain. She assumed that the girl had had to leave the *parador* because of her brother's behavior and that Don Rafael had offered her asylum at Las Aguilas when he found her stranded. Rosalie thought she must be either blind or stupid to accept such an explanation. To start with, Don Rafael was not a philanthropist, but it made the position more pleasant to preserve this fiction, and the woman's desire for Rosalie's company seemed perfectly genuine.

"I like young people around me when they are well behaved," she told her. "You are neither rowdy nor restless, *niña.* I will not pretend that life at the Casa Blanca will be exciting, there will be no parties or entertainments, but you will find plenty of subjects to paint, and perhaps Don Rafael will show you some of the places of interest."

Rosalie insisted that she would be content with a quiet life and was grateful for the chance to see more of Spain.

"*Bueno,* and I am grateful to you," the Condesa said graciously, "and who knows, our connection may become permanent."

Rosalie did not think she would want to remain with Doña Teresa indefinitely, but now was not the time to say so. Her new employer was smiling at her indulgently, but the smile did not reach her eyes. Meeting them, Rosalie surprised such a look of calculated cunning that she was momentarily repelled. Then the Condesa picked up her needlework and began to discuss the details of their journey. She looked so guileless that Rosalie decided she must have imagined that strange expression. The Condesa was only a harmless old woman who was pleased to have secured the services of a youthful companion.

CHAPTER FIVE

ROSALIE ANSWERED Philip's letter, telling him that she was sorry she could not come to his wedding but she had had the chance of a congenial position that entailed traveling south immediately, and she did not think she would be missed. In any case she had no suitable clothes. As soon as she had a settled address, she would send him a postcard. She did not mention her employer's name, and that she thought would have to do for the present. Later when she had reached Andalusia, she would write more fully and try to elucidate the whereabouts of the bracelet, for she was determined that somehow it must be returned to the Santaellas.

In more normal circumstances, nothing would have prevented her from attending her twin's wedding, but Philip had issued such a casual invitation that it hardly amounted to one, and his complete disregard of the financial difficulties involved had wounded her; nor could she overlook that he was, as Don Rafael had pointed out, subsisting upon the sale of the diamonds.

She needed to get her letter mailed and wondered if the Santaellas would raise any objection. Don Rafael appeared to be resigned to the situation, but he was unpredictable. She was still at a loss to account for the extraordinary way he had exploded when he had told her to get out. The only explanation seemed to be that he feared she was going to upset his plans. He had decided she would be useful as a companion for his mother and was annoyed when he thought she wanted to go to Paris, but that was a poor excuse for such a burst of fury. She hoped she would not provoke another one when she told him she had written to her brother.

The mail was collected when the postman delivered, and letters were left ready for him in the great hall. If he did not call, Jacobo would send one of his grandsons with it to the village.

Determined not to descend to subterfuge, she said at breakfast, "I've answered Phil's letter. I suppose you've no objection?"

"I hope you've told him you intend to stay in Spain," the Condesa said anxiously.

"Yes, and that I've changed my job, but I didn't mention any names."

Rafael and his mother exchanged glances, and he laughed.

"Very discreet of you," he approved. "If you give me your missive, I myself will mail it. I am going down to the village," Then seeing her hesitation, he added, "Unless you would prefer to mail it yourself, but the road as you know is very hot and dusty and not entirely safe for women alone."

Rosalie dropped her eyes, unable to meet the mischief in his, and Doña Teresa said repressively, "Nonsense, the road is perfectly safe, but it is not fitting that you should wander about alone."

A reminder that she was about to become the Condesa's staid companion, conforming to Spanish rules of conduct, and that Rafael would never kiss her again. She ought to be thankful for her changed status, but perversely she was regretful. That brought her up

against something that she did not want to examine
too closely. Her enthusiasm for Andalusia, her grati-
tude to Doña Teresa were superficial emotions
imposed upon something much stronger. Underlying
them was an intense relief that she would not have to
say goodbye to Rafael and for some weeks at least she
would still be under his roof. She pushed the realiza-
tion deep down into her subconscious, for that the
insolent, demanding Spaniard had made an impression upon her heart was a ludicrous supposition.
Unfortunately her body betrayed her; she could not
encounter him unexpectedly without a leap of the
heart, and his proximity affected her nerves to an
alarming extent. Furiously she insisted to herself that
it was the aftermath of his bullying behavior on that
first day, but that did not explain why she had been so
loath to go home and her pleasure in her reprieve.

The envelope she handed to Don Rafael was
inscribed with her mother's Parisian address, but that
did not matter now. She was confident Don Rafael
had abandoned his search for Philip and Consuelo.

"There is something I must return to you before we
leave," he told her, slipping the missive into his pocket.
"Come into my *oficina*." This bare little room was
where he kept his safe, and unlocking it, he handed her
an envelope containing her passport and money.

"Do you not wish to count it?" he asked, as she
stuffed it into her handbag. "This rapacious Spaniard
may have robbed you."

"I'm sure you would never do that," she returned.

"Do not be too sure," he told her with an enigmatic
smile. "A few pesetas are no temptation, but on larger
issues. . . ." He broke off, shrugging his shoulders.
"Possibly you would like to do a little shopping when
we stop in Cordoba?"

"Yes, I need some more artists' materials," she said eagerly.

"*Claro*, such dedication!"

She guessed he had expected her to want to buy fripperies, but she did not want to waste money on unessentials.

She went back to join her new employer and help with the preparations for their departure. They were to start early the next morning.

The journey was to her one of sheer enchantment. Rosalie traveled in the back of Rafael's ageing but still serviceable car, while the Condesa sat beside her son. The dreary dun-colored plains were left behind when they reached the ragged battlements of the Sierra Morena. The sides of the Gorge of Despenaperros, which was the way through the mountains, were covered with flowers that resembled wild roses, among which the bees were busy. *Romero*, Doña Teresa said the bloom was called, and *romero*-flavored honey was a speciality of the region. The road descended to the plain where there were asphodels, acanthus and aspidistras. The first cactuses appeared, aloes and prickly ears, under a deep blue sky. It was intensely hot. Rafael stopped for a long cool drink at a whitewalled *posada* with its sunblinds drawn. Fuchsias, geraniums and ferns filled its windowboxes and stood in pots along its walls. Rosalie felt that at last she was seeing what she had thought of as Spain.

Cordoba appeared on the horizon, visible several miles away.

It had been the capital of the old Moorish Caliphate and was built upon the banks of the Guadalquivir. The river divides the province, the mining and stockbreeding zones being to the hilly north, the agricultural

lands to the south. Don Rafael drove through the sub-
urbs, over the Roman bridge and into the heart of the
city, because he said their visitor ought to see a real
Andalusian town. He pointed out the cathedral, still
called the Mosque, but said they hadn't the time to go
inside it; he also pointed out the Alcazar and various
other buildings of interest in the old part of the town.
There seemed to be Gothic churches named for every
saint, including San Rafael for whom Santaella was
called.

Finally he parked among the modern shops and
insisted upon accompanying Rosalie to make her pur-
chases in case she had difficulty with the language.
Doña Teresa left them to it, going off on some errand
of her own.

Rosalie spent recklessly, for her art was to be her
main diversion during her stay. Hitherto she had
worked with pencil and felt pens when she needed col-
or, for she had been unable to carry much with her. To
her dismay, Rafael paid the bill, which the assistant
presented to him as a matter of course.

"I must pay you back," she said, fumbling with her
bag as they left the shop, Rafael carrying her parcel.

"*Absurdo.* This—" he tapped the parcel "—will, I
hope, keep you quiet and contented and that is worth
the expenditure of a few pesetas."

A few! It had been several hundred.

The Casa Blanca was situated to the south of the
city in the rich lands of the Campina region. It was
charming. As its name implied it was white with the
typical wrought-iron *rejas* and balconies and built
around a patio bright with flowers. Rosalie's room had
a little balcony, full of potted plants, overlooking the
patio. Bougainvilleas, oleanders and other subtropical
shrubs enclosed the whole edifice in a scented bower.

Inside, the long, low-ceilinged rooms were dim and cool, even in the full heat of summer, for the walls were thick and venetian blinds were drawn over the windows.

Rosalie found her duties not at all arduous. They consisted mainly of being there so that the Condesa had someone to whom to talk. While she drew and painted and the Condesa sewed, the latter enlarged upon her country's history and customs and was lavish with her information. She also took Rosalie's Spanish in hand, insisting that she must speak the language like a Castilian, though all the people around them used the Andaluz patois. She declared that she must also be able to write it. Sometimes it seemed to Rosalie that she was more like a governess than an employer, but she supposed that it amused her to act as a teacher. It never occurred to her that there might be a reason for all this intensive instruction.

Of Rafael Rosalie did not see a great deal. He was out in the mornings before she came down from the breakfast that was brought to her room by one of the maids, of which there were several, labor being cheap in that province, and often did not come in all day. Very occasionally he joined them for their midday meal, but dinner, which appeared about ten o'clock, was the only time when they met regularly, and sometimes he would sit with them in the patio afterward while they took their coffee. Even then he was usually withdrawn, though Rosalie often found his dark eyes watching her with a speculative look. She liked having him there where she could eye him furtively from under her long lashes and listen to his deep voice while he talked to his mother in sonorous Spanish, only half of which she could understand. The Condesa insisted that he should not speak English or Rosalie would never become fluent in their tongue. Being uncertain of her own proficiency in it, she seldom spoke, and he rarely addressed her directly. He seemed to wish to emphasize that it was solely on his mother's account that she was there, and if that was the way he wanted it, she had no intention of trying to attract his notice. Nor did he show any interest in her artistic efforts, though the Condesa occasionally asked her to display her work. Rosalie would hand him some innocuous study of trees or plants, and he would compliment her perfunctorily.

It was during the golden afternoons, while the Condesa took her siesta, that Rosalie did her real work, the imaginative forerunners of the pictures she hoped one day to reproduce in oils. They depicted dramatic landscapes with fretted peaks, the Sierra Morena, or stretches of barren sun-struck plain surrounding a ruined castle. Only rough sketches as yet, but containing the germ of genius that would one day flower.

She favored browns, blacks and ocher, with occasional splashes of scarlet to color her impressions of the harsh, cruel land of the black legend, scarred by the pitiless elements. Her imagination found it more inspiring than the more obvious beauty of the south, which had already been so often immortalized.

She was creating a background for her central figure and that was to be that of a man who had no softness in his makeup, who was ruthless, strong and arrogant and who would epitomize the very soul of Spain. Though only outlines appeared on her paper, the features were clearly recognizable, in profile, full face and three-quarters, the proud, aloof face she was able to study every evening. She had often drawn the Condesa, who was so like him, but her masterpiece, if she ever were able to realize her dream, would be that of the man alone, a stark, lonely figure, arresting in its simplicity.

She worked in the watercolors and crayons she had bought in Cordoba, the paraphernalia necessary for oil painting being too bulky to accommodate at the Casa, but the finished product would be in oils.

While she worked, she dreamed, not realizing that an obsession with the living man was the root of her creation; or if she dimly sensed it, she knew he was too far beyond her reach to accept him on a man-woman basis. It was enough that if she fulfilled her ambitions, she would immortalize him with her talent.

So the timeless, sunbaked days passed slowly until Eloisa Carvello descended upon the Casa Blanca, shattering its peace and serenity with the impact of a bomb.

She drove up one afternoon at the end of the siesta hour. Rafael for once had come in for lunch, and had lingered to let the heat abate. He and the two women were on the patio, Doña Teresa busy with her embroidery silks, while Rosalie was studying a Spanish grammar book and covertly watching Rafael, as he lounged half-asleep in a canvas chair, smoking a cheroot. His Cordoban hat lay discarded beside him, his shirt collar was open, with a twist of scarlet scarf about his throat, his long legs clad in breeches and boots, for he kept a horse at Casa Blanca and would be riding around the estate as soon as it was cooler. He looked alluring, masculine and remote.

The sound of the car was audible from the patio, so also a woman's shrill voice, inquiring if the Condesa was at home.

Rafael's black brows descended at the sound of it.

"*Mal suerte*," he growled, "I should have been on my way. Now it is too late."

Doña Teresa glanced at him meaningly.

"I hear Señor Carvello prospers nowadays. Eloisa will have a substantial dowry."

"*Por Dios*, from Consuelo to that is a long step down!"

But his manner was courteous, even charming as the visitor was ushered into the patio.

Eloisa Carvello was small and plump with a round face, beady black eyes and smooth dark hair, reminding Rosalie of a Dutch doll. What she lacked in personal distinction she made up for in her clothes. Rosalie saw the Condesa look quizzically at the very short scarlet skirt, transparent blouse and black sleeveless jacket. She sat down in the chair Rafael set for her, crossing silken legs and thus revealing far more of them than seemed proper. Rosalie noticed Rafael glance at them with a smile, while he poured her a glass of cognac. Disdaining the usual Sangria, she had asked for spirits.

"I like something with a kick in it," she had said, and Doña Teresa looked disapproving. But she inquired politely about the girl's family. Apparently she had parents and a brother living with her. Their estate was not far away, and Señor Carvello grew oranges and vines, but now he was launching out into a hotel.

Rosalie was introduced to her by Doña Teresa as, "An English girl who took pity on my loneliness and is spending the summer with me."

Eloisa gave the English girl a contemptuous stare.

"You are fortunate, *señorita*," she said coldly. "The Casa Blanca is a delightful place to spend a summer," and from thenceforth ignored her, chattering away in Spanish.

"You have kept your arrival very quiet," she said to Rafael. "It is only by chance that Luis discovered you were here. I came at once to pay my respects and to tell you that Papa has opened a guest house since you were last here. We now have a swimming pool and a tennis court you must come and sample."

"I am a very busy man," he returned, "and have little time for such amusements. Besides, surely these amenities are intended for your patrons?"

"We are not very full at the moment," Eloisa admitted. "But it is only our first season and no one is more welcome than you."

"Thank you, but I have no great love for the society of foreign riffraff," he told her with a touch of disdain. "And I see you are already copying their habits." He eyed her legs. "I am surprised your father allows you to run about the country alone."

She laughed gaily, quite unabashed.

"We must move with the times, Don Rafael, and we girls are not longer content to sit at home twiddling our thumbs waiting for husbands to be found for us."

"You prefer to go and hunt for them yourselves?"

She laughed again, but a little uncertainly.

"You are pleased to joke, Don Rafael, but yes, the foreign girls have shown us a thing or two."

"So I perceive," he returned dryly.

"The day of the *duena* is over," she declared dramatically.

The Condesa said, "What does your mother think about these innovations?"

Eloisa shrugged and smiled. "I have not asked her, but I can guess. She is old-fashioned."

Don Rafael rose to his feet and apologized for having to go.

"Duty calls. I have to superintend the spraying of some fruit trees."

Eloisa jumped up. "Let me come with you. There has been much talk of this spraying of trees and I would like to tell my father how it is done."

Rafael's smile was saturnine. "Quite the farmer's daughter, but I was going to ride."

"Is it too far to walk? I can follow you with my car. Or better still, drive you to wherever it is."

"*Bueno*, that is an excellent idea. I shall be honored with your company."

He stood aside to let her pass, but she halted by his side, slipping her arm through his and looking up into his unresponsive face.

"We have kindred interests, have we not?" she said provocatively and lightly tapped his cheek. "Do not look so solemn, *amigo*. I prefer you when you smile."

They left the patio and the Condesa looked at Rosalie.

"Brazen hussy," she said calmly. "In the old days if a girl permitted a man to so much as touch her she was considered unfit to be a wife and mother. Eloisa must have heard of Consuelo's elopement and hopes to catch Rafael on the rebound." She threaded a needle deliberately. "She might be quite a good match."

"But I thought you had already selected a candidate," Rosalie said, surprised. "I mean . . . Don Rafael did mention something about some foreign girl."

"How very indiscreet, and to you of all people!" Doña Teresa exclaimed. She regarded Rosalie meditatively. "It is true I had someone in mind, but on second thoughts, Eloisa might be an easier proposition, and she is Spanish."

"And is Don Rafael content for you to choose his wife?" Rosalie asked, stung out of caution by her indignation at such indifference on Rafael's part toward the woman he was to marry.

"It is usual for the parents to arrange marriages in Spain," the Condesa said calmly. "Or rather I should say, it was usual. As Eloisa has been telling us we are entering upon a new era. I will admit that Eloisa Carvello is not my choice for a daughter-in-law—her people are what you call jumped up, and she has no modesty and no dignity—but if she can console my poor son for his disappointment, I shall not oppose their union."

The glance she gave Rosalie was definitely sly, and the girl winced inwardly. Did the Condesa imagine that she herself was cherishing a yen for Rafael?

"I'm sure I hope she can," she said carelessly.

"How generous of you," the Condesa observed ambiguously, and Rosalie flushed. Hastily she began to talk about something else.

Naturally an adoring mother would expect any young woman to be attracted to her son, but really, thought Rosalie, Don Rafael's matrimonial concerns were of no interest to her whatever. He was an arrogant Spaniard and not the type of man who would appeal to her at all, but—and here her reflections wavered—he did have a strange sort of fascination, and he had impressed his image upon her imagination very thoroughly. She remembered guiltily all the drawings she had made of him and the disturbing effect he so often had upon her, but that meant nothing. It was a girl's natural reaction to a good-looking man, and she studied him only because she found him so inspiring, the ideal model for her Spanish pictures. All the same, she felt uncomfortable under the Condesa's quizzical regard. A three-cornered situation with herself and Eloisa competing for Rafael's favors was one that would appeal to the older woman, and she had no intention of providing her with that sort of entertainment.

Cutting into Rosalie's thoughts, Doña Teresa remarked, "Eloisa was angling for Don Rafael all last summer, but she did not make much headway, for he preferred Consuelo, so perhaps my original plan will be best. It was I, you know, who suggested that match to Señor Nuñez. It seemed such a good idea." She sighed.

"Then I wish you better success with your next one," Rosalie told her a little tartly.

"I am sure I will have," the Condesa returned, beaming at her.

Eloisa prolonged her stay until dusk was falling. She was endeavoring to persuade the Santaellas to visit her father's guest house, of which Don Rafael could barely conceal his disapproval. She found an unexpected ally in the Condesa, who announced that she would like to see the place, and of course Rosalie must accompany her.

"*Claro*," Eloisa agreed unwillingly, adding spitefully, "If you feel you will need her support."

Rafael said, "Then you will not need my escort, mama. I will drop you there and come to fetch you."

Eloisa protested loudly and again the Condesa came to her assistance.

"That would not be very courteous to Señor and Señora Carvello," she pointed out. "I am sure you can spare one day from your labors, Rafael."

Her son looked at her with a slightly puzzled expression. He knew she did not like Eloisa's family and was at a loss to account for her acceptance, but in view of her rebuke he had no option but to fall in with her wishes.

When Eloisa had gone after fixing a day and an hour, he asked, "Why do you wish to encourage these people, mama? I am amazed that you want to visit this *posada* that Carvello has made his latest investment."

"I have my reasons," Doña Teresa told him, but did not divulge what they were. In spite of what she had said previously, Rosalie concluded that she was seriously considering Eloisa as a successor to Consuelo, or perhaps she only wished to keep her in reserve in case her other negotiations fell through. She had no desire to have any further contact with that young woman herself, and requested that she might be allowed to stay behind.

"That would not do at all," her employer objected. "I shall require your presence to sustain me among the *turistas*."

"You will be more at home with them than we shall be," Rafael told her, "after your time at the *parador*."

Rosalie was about to say that there she had been in a rather different position, but checked herself in time. For her position was not greatly different, for she was still an employee—that Eloisa had guessed at once. Her manner had shown it. As such she must concur with Doña Teresa's orders, and once she got there she must expect to be ignored.

That did not prove to be the case. The Carvellos had erected a huge white building amid their orange groves. It was in the same style as the hotels along the coast, though they advertised it as a select retreat amid the peace of the countryside for those who sought refuge from the crowds of tourists. Though it did not have the lure of the sea, there were mountains not far away and it was within easy reach of Cordoba. Señor Carvello had provided facilities for riding, built a large swimming pool and laid out tennis courts. There was even a golf course where the hills began a short distance away.

Señor Carvello was a short rotund man who greeted his august guests with deference. He was bursting with pride in his new achievement.

"Already we have many bookings for the holiday season," he said happily. "Many family parties with *los niños*. You should cash in while you can, Conde, on the tourist boom. That *castillo* of yours would make a fine hotel."

"I have not the capital to convert it," Rafael said shortly.

"But loans can be raised. . . . " The other man raised his head haughtily, and Señor Carvello subsided. "You know your own business best," he muttered.

"I certainly do," Rafael informed him.

The Condesa was settled in the shade by the side of the swimming pool where deck chairs and loungers were set out. Eloisa began to badger Rafael to sample the pool.

"And the Señorita Smith also," suggested her brother, Luis. He had joined them at the pool's edge, already dressed, or rather undressed, in a pair of swimming trunks. He was a slight, bronzed young man, very little taller than Rosalie. He was much better-looking than his sister and had startlingly blue eyes in a thin brown face. Some legacy from a Castilian forebear, thought Rosalie.

"I haven't brought a swimsuit," Rosalie said, seeking to excuse herself.

"One can be found for you, I am sure," Luis insisted.

"Thank you, *señor*, but I prefer to stay with the Condesa."

"*Absurdo*," that lady said vigorously. "I have brought you here to enjoy yourself, not to wait upon me." She then proceeded to direct operations. Eloisa unwillingly produced a suit, not a bikini but a discreet one-piece affair in dark green, to Rosalie's relief. She had no wish to make herself conspicuous, or offend the Condesa's old-fashioned ideas. She was not an expert swimmer, as she told Luis when she came out of the changing room and found him waiting for her.

"Then it will be my privilege to make you become so," he said gallantly, looking appreciatively at her long limbs. "Trust yourself to me, *señorita*, and I will permit none of the show-offs to submerge you."

Rosalie wondered if he were referring to Rafael, who was already in the pool with Eloisa, the only other occupants being a couple of middle-aged men who did not look enterprising. He was shooting down its full length under water, and when he emerged at the end she saw he was wearing a complete bathing costume. She remembered that such a style was favored in Spain instead of trunks only, though the convention was rapidly being ignored by the younger men. He climbed up on the diving board, a lean brown and black figure, and then swooped back into the water like a swallow.

Eloisa, clad in the scantiest of bikinis, was holding on to the handrail and kicking at the shallow end. She could not swim. She called to Rafael to come and support her out into the middle of the pool, which he did unwillingly, amid much squealing on the girl's part, to the amusement of the onlookers sitting around the water. Rafael was not amused and was scowling as he towed Eloisa into deeper water. Seeing his expression, Rosalie thought the Spanish girl was being foolhardy. He looked quite capable of deliberately ducking her.

Soon, however, her whole attention was claimed by Luis, who, after she had done her modest breaststroke across the pool, insisted that she try something more ambitious. It was pleasantly cool in the water, which was shaded by the surrounding palms and tamarisks, and there was no mistaking the honest admiration in Luis's eyes. In spite of the opportunities her tuition gave him, he did not take advantage of them, and Rosalie began to enjoy herself. When she began to tire, Luis guided her to the steps and springing up ahead of her, held out his hand to give her unneeded assistance. Still retaining her hand, he led her to two chairs set a little apart from the others, and found for her a voluminous towel. The sunlight dripped through the trees in golden spotlights as she rubbed her wet head— Eloisa had not provided a cap—finding threads of shining copper among the brown. Unasked, Luis offered her a comb, and sinking into the chair beside her regarded her appraisingly.

"*Muy guapa*," was his verdict.

With a flash of memory she recalled where she had last heard those words. She had been insolently accosted upon a dusty road, and a short while later imprisoned by a pair of sinewy arms. Her eyes sought for Rafael in the pool. He was standing waist deep, holding Eloisa by her middle, and she was kicking and squealing.

Luis moved uncomfortably.

"My sister makes her desires too obvious," he said distastefully.

"She seems to be enjoying herself," Rosalie observed.

"Enjoyment can be bought too dear," he told her. He looked at her languishingly. "But look at me, not at them. Tell me all about yourself and how you come to be here."

An awkward question to answer truthfully. She said frankly that she had always wanted to visit Spain but could only do so if she worked. At present she was the Condesa's companion and considered herself lucky to have obtained such an easy job. Reminded of her employer, she looked across to the opposite side of the pool where the Condesa was sitting and saw she was watching them with a little satisfied smile. Far from disapproving, she seemed pleased that Rosalie had found an admirer. Whatever doubts she might have about Eloisa's suitability for her son, a Carvello was quite good enough for her companion.

"What are you thinking about so seriously, *amiga*?" Luis asked. "I do not think you have heard what I have been saying."

Rosalie blushed guiltily. "Sorry," she apologized. "I was half asleep. What was it?"

His eyes were reproachful. "You find me tedious?"

"Not in the least." She made an effort to rouse herself. "You've made my day. But for you I'd be sitting over there beside the Condesa, looking on."

"I think you have done too much looking on at life. It is time you took an active part in it." He leaned toward her and his blue eyes became ardent. "Let me teach you how to live."

"Señor Carvello!" She drew back in her chair. "We have only met this afternoon."

"My name is Luis," he reminded her, "and I find you *simpática*. I feel as if I had known you all my life, Rosa." She smiled at this extravagance. "Your name is Rosa, is it not? I heard the Condesa call you so."

"Actually it's Rosalie."

"I prefer Rosa, for you are like a rose, your petals still curled about your heart. I would penetrate to that heart, Rosa *mia.*"

"Very pretty and flowery, but aren't you going rather too fast for a Spaniard? I've always understood their approach was much more leisurely and formal."

He smiled. "It certainly is. Spanish courtship old style follows a formula. It is like a quadrille, a series of set positions."

"Tell me how it goes," she prompted, as he paused.

"You want to know? *Bien*, it is this way: the start, he stares at her in church; two, at the *reja* he sighs; three, he is allowed to take her to the movies perhaps and it is permissible to hold her hand—for three minutes only. Then follow the set speeches, arranged in order of increasing fervor, to be delivered on schedule over a period of six months. The girl knows the drill as well as he does, and if he omits one step, she decides he is lacking in ardor."

"What a drawn-out process!"

"It is, and of no use with girls who are only here on a two-week vacation. There is no time for set speeches."

"But I shall be here for longer than two weeks."

"Then do you wish me to embark upon the whole procedure?"

She shook her head. "I wouldn't care for set speeches. I would doubt their sincerity."

"Ah, but you must not doubt mine, and I have

adapted to more modern methods. Life is too short for drawn-out courtship."

Rosalie lay back in her chair and smiled provocatively. It was very pleasant to be able to flirt with a personable young man; it was a pleasure that had been denied to her for far too long.

" 'Gather ye rosebuds while ye may, old time is still a-flying,' " she quoted.

"An excellent sentiment. How long do you expect to be in Andalusia, Rosa?"

"For some time yet, I hope."

He leaned toward her again, blue eyes intent.

"Will there be time to gather my rosebud, Rosa?"

"Señorita Smith, it is time you dressed yourself," a cold voice said. "We must return home."

Rosalie had been so engrossed in her conversation with Luis that she had not noticed Rafael's approach. He was standing before her fully dressed and there was disapproval in every line of his taut body.

She sprang to her feet. "I'm sorry, Don Rafael, I didn't realize—"

He cut through her words. "That is obvious. The Condesa is waiting for you."

Glancing guiltily across the pool, she saw that Doña Teresa's chair was vacant.

"I'll be as quick as I can," she stammered and fled toward the changing room.

When she returned, Eloisa and Luis were both urging the Conde and Condesa to stay for dinner, and Señor Carvello waddled up to add his persuasions to theirs. He desired to show off the excellence of his chef, but Rafael was adamant.

"My mother is tired," he stated. "She goes out so seldom that she must not overdo it."

"Then could not the Señorita Smith stay?" Luis asked. "I will bring her back."

This suggestion met with a glacial reception both from his father and the two guests.

"We know the Señorita is English," Rafael said coldly, "but while she is under my roof she will adhere to our ways."

"The old ways?" Luis queried, looking unpleasant. "Times change, Don Rafael."

"Not with me they don't," the Conde snapped. He took his mother's arm. "Precede us to the car, Señorita Smith."

Feeling in disgrace, Rosalie smiled at Luis and walked with what dignity she could muster to the waiting vehicle. She experienced a surge of resentment against Don Rafael. Even if he did employ her, he had no right to treat her like a naughty child because she had enjoyed a few minutes' conversation with a boy who treated her like a human being. A few minutes? She noticed how the shadows had lengthened since she had come out of the pool. She had been talking to Luis for quite a time, and wearing only her swimsuit. That, she supposed, was another offense.

Luis shot forward to open the rear door for her, while his parents who had come to see them off looked on. Rosalie turned back to add her thanks to the Condesa's for a pleasant afternoon, but aware of their stony regard and Don Rafael's black looks, wished she hadn't bothered.

She stepped into the car and Luis put his head in to whisper, "They are a lot of spoilsports. *Hasta la vista*, Rosa." He smiled and touched her hand.

Don Rafael slid into the driver's seat and slammed the door. Luis closed the rear door more gently and stepped back. The car moved away and Rosalie started to apologize to the Condesa for her neglect.

"It is nothing, *chica*. I am glad you had a good time," Doña Teresa said graciously. She glanced at her son's set face, a triumphant little smile edging her lips. "Luis Carvello is a great improvement upon his sister."

Rosalie sat back in her seat feeling nonplussed. Whatever gaffe she had committed, if she had committed one, it had not offended the Condesa, but it had definitely offended Don Rafael. Again she felt resentful, recalling his behavior with Eloisa in the pool. Like so many men of his kind he made one law for his women and another for himself. She recalled that she had read somewhere that the more a man indulged in his amorous fancies, the more particular he was about his own family's conduct. But she was no kin of his; she had come upon this expedition only at his mother's insistence, and he could have easily prevented it. If the outcome had displeased him, he had only himself to blame. If Luis Carvello sought her out, and she suspected that he meant to do so, she would welcome him, and if Don Rafael didn't like it, that would be just too bad—for him.

Rosalie settled herself in her seat, allowing herself to relax, and watched the purple shadows creep over the Andalusian plain, heralding the coming night. The penetrating scent of the *dama de noche*, a succulent plant, was wafted in the open car windows.

In this most romantic land, she could not be expected to forgo romance!

CHAPTER SIX

ALL THROUGH DINNER upon their return, Don Rafael was moody and taciturn. Doña Teresa, on the other hand, was almost sprightly. It seemed that her son's ill humor was diverting her, though Rosalie could not imagine why. Their neighbors' venture into the hotel business brought forth some acid remarks.

"But he will make a go of it," Doña Teresa decided. "Everything that man touches succeeds."

"Very estimable, but he seems unable to protect his daughter's honor," Rafael announced censoriously. "She will bring shame upon him if she continues as she is doing."

"What would you do if she were yours?" his mother inquired.

"Subject her to the old rules, which are best in the long run. No bikinis, no staying out late, and kept closely guarded at home."

"But that's ridiculous!" Rosalie exclaimed, roused out of her usual submissiveness by this tyrannical decree. "Because the Señorita follows modern trends, it doesn't mean that she's bad."

"She gives the appearance of being so, which is worse."

"Oh, really!" Rosalie felt helpless before such reasoning.

"You are prejudiced, my son," the Condesa told him. "Eloisa has more sense than to ruin herself, she is only inaugurating the New Spain." She put her head on one side, pensively regarding Don Rafael. "That hotel will be a money-spinner. I think you should seriously consider an alliance with Eloisa."

Rafael muttered something uncomplimentary about the girl.

"You cannot have everything," the Condesa pointed out, "I daresay you can manage to check that irritating giggle and insist upon a little more decorous behavior, *mi hijo,* and her pesetas will bring the Castillo back to prosperity."

She seemed to be deliberately trying to push the girl on to her son, while his reluctance amused her.

"I am not sure I shall retain Las Aguilas," Rafael said. "Andalusia suits me better." He glanced obliquely at Rosalie.

The Condesa looked perturbed.

"But it is the cradle of your race, Rafael. There you were born, and your father before you. Its ownership enhances your prestige. Casa Blanca is only a farm."

"I am still a Santaella wherever I am," he retorted proudly. "And whatever I do." He rose abruptly from the table. "Señorita Smith, when you have finished, will you be so good as to join me in my *oficino*? I have something that I wish to say to you."

Rosalie glanced in consternation at the Condesa.

"Can't you say it here?" she asked uncertainly.

"No." He was curt.

"Very well, *señor,*" she agreed meekly, but she did not hurry over her dessert and continued to dissect the peach she was eating with outward calm and inward trepidation.

When he had gone, she said to Doña Teresa, "I haven't done anything wrong, have I?"

"Far from it, *chica*," the Condesa assured her with a twinkle in her dark eyes.

"He seemed annoyed with me this afternoon."

"Not at all, Rosa. You merely presented him with an ultimatum."

"I'm sure I did no such thing. I don't understand you, madam."

"All will become clear in due course."

Rosalie gave it up. "But why does he want to speak to me?" she asked.

"That you will soon find out."

Rosalie rose reluctantly from the table.

"Well, I'd better get it over with."

Rafael's office, like the one in the Castillo, was a small, bare room, but with a pleasant view onto the patio. Here he kept the papers pertaining to the estate. It contained a large flat table he used as a desk, a filing cabinet, a swivel chair, in which he was sitting, and several hard upright ones. The light above spilled over his blue black hair and accentuated the narrow planes of his face. He seemed absorbed in the spread of papers before him.

Rosalie paused in the doorway, having entered at his response to her knock. At first she did not take in what it was he was studying so closely, and then she saw with near horror that the contents of her portfolio were spread before him and he was examining each sketch with meticulous care. How had he obtained them? She was always careful to put them away in her room, especially the ones she did not want him to see. Dismay was succeeded by a rush of indignation. He had no right to look at them without her permission. They were as private as her letters. He was violating the sanctuary of her most intimate secrets.

Advancing toward the table, she demanded, "Where did you find those? I'm sure I left them in my room. Did you dare to take them?"

He stood up and indicated a chair.

"Please sit down, *señorita.*"

She remained standing, saying stormily, "You haven't answered my question!"

"My mother gave them to me," he returned mildly. "She greatly admires your talent, and she thinks it is a great pity that you should not have more training. In fact she has suggested that you might like to take lessons while you are here. There are several well-known artists in the vicinity who might take you as a pupil. Naturally I wished to judge for myself of you capabilities, having seen but little of your work, before arranging anything. So she handed me your portfolio."

Rosalie subsided into the chair he had indicated, momentarily bereft of speech. His explanation was reasonable and presumably his mother did not regard her work as private, but he could not fail to recognize the repetition of his own features she had so faithfully portrayed, not only in her earlier flight of imagination—the *conquistador* and the *grandee*—but in her more advanced compositions, forerunners of the oil paintings she wanted one day to make of them. She glanced at his enigmatic face out of the corner of her eye. He did not seem annoyed, so possibly he had not recognized himself.

He had resumed his seat and was calmly shuffling through the sheets of drawing paper, while he remarked drily, "You seem best at portraiture, but you have suffered from a scarcity of models. Perhaps you found fresh inspiration among the people you met today. I am sure Luis Carvello would be pleased to sit for you."

Relieved that he did not consider she had been impertinent and was disregarding the personal aspect, she said truthfully, "I didn't find his features very interesting."

"Now you do surprise me." He sat back, twirling his chair from side to side, while he stared at her across the table. "You find mine more so?"

Rosalie flushed and looked down at her hands clasped in her lap.

"From an artist's standpoint, yes," she told him composedly. "They have more character."

He picked up her sketch of the *conquistador* and regarded it with a satirical smile.

"So I was a model for your idea of Pizarro and Cortez. Ruthless men, Rosa."

Though his mother called her Rosa, he was usually more formal, and the sound of her name on his lips gave her an unexpected dart of pleasure.

"Well, weren't they?" she countered.

"Very. Do you consider me ruthless, too?"

"I know you can be."

"Then it would be wise not to provoke me."

"I always endeavor not to do so."

"Don't be mealy-mouthed with me, Rosa. It does not suit you." He pushed her drawings aside, and proceeded to light a cheroot. Through the cloud of blue smoke he looked at her keenly.

"You seemed to have a lot to say to that young man this afternoon; in fact, when I interrupted you, it appeared to me that you were leading him on."

Rosalie made an effort to meet his eyes, and instantly looked down again. His were not disapproving as she had expected, but held the slumbrous sensual expression she always found so intensely disturbing. Her stomach fluttered and her heartbeat quickened.

"Was that what you wanted to see me about—the drawing lessons, I mean?" she asked, striving to keep her voice steady. She ignored the subject of Luis, and as he did not immediately reply, she went on rapidly, "It is most kind of you to think of obtaining a teacher for me, but if he's a good artist, he would be very expensive."

"His fees would be my business."

"But I couldn't allow—"

"I shall insist."

She laughed. "Really, Don Rafael, you've changed in an extraordinary degree since our first meeting. Who would have dreamed then that you would end up by offering me art lessons?"

"Ah, but this is not the end, it is the beginning."

She flashed a look at him only to meet that disconcerting expression.

"I . . . I don't understand," she faltered.

"It occurs to me that time lies heavy on your hands, so I am proposing to arrange a more suitable occupation for you than flirting with youthful upstarts."

The insolence of his tone fired her.

"A bribe, in fact," she exclaimed scornfully. "To make me conform to your outdated notions of propriety. Luis Carvello is a nice boy and I like him. If you think you've a right to censor my friendships because your mother employs me, you've another thing coming, Don Rafael. We're not in your medieval fortress now, and I refuse to be bullied and coerced. I have no intention of dropping Luis, and if the Condesa wishes to dispense with my services upon such a flimsy pretext, I must accept my dismissal. I daresay I can find other employment."

"I admire your spirit but not your wisdom," he told her, tight-lipped. "To throw up a good position for the sake of a pair of blue eyes is not sensible."

Rosalie rose to her feet, instinctively wanting to put distance between them. She had received an impression of leashed violence in the man before her, which might be loosed at any moment. She did not really care if she never saw Luis again, and she was being foolish to jeopardize her position in this pleasant household over such an unimportant issue; but she was dimly aware that it went much deeper than that. From their first meeting Don Rafael had sought to dominate her for one reason or another, and her independence was at stake. She was not going to allow him to dictate to her.

"Sit down," he commanded. "I have not finished."

"I think you've said plenty," she returned. "I don't want to hear any more."

She moved toward the door, which was a mistake, for her intention of escaping aroused his hunting instinct. With the swift lithe movement of a predatory animal, he pounced. She was held against his chest, unable to defend herself, while his mouth sought hers, and with a little gasp Rosalie surrendered. In a moment of blinding illumination she knew that this was that for which she had been secretly yearning.

He kissed her eyelids, her throat and her mouth again. His fingers sought the zipper of her dress, pulling it down so that her neck and shoulders were exposed to his fierce caresses. Finally, with obvious reluctance, he dropped her back onto her chair and turned away, breathing fast.

Mechanically Rosalie adjusted her dress. She had been taken completely by surprise, not only by his ardor but by her own reaction to it.

She knew she had responded shamelessly to his passion, and a whole new world was unfolding before her hitherto limited experience. She had never before been stirred by such a tumult of emotion.

Rafael came back to her, his eyes glowing.

"That will make you forget that young cub!"

With a surge of triumph she realized that what had motivated him throughout the interview was jealousy of the other man.

But as her racing pulses slowed, she looked askance at him. What was to happen now? In the castle she had feared his intentions, but then she had seen him as an embittered and vengeful tyrant. Now her own feelings were involved, and she was more in his power than she had been then, for she doubted that she would be able to resist him.

Rafael seated himself on the edge of the table, swinging one foot. He looked much younger, even boyish, his eyes still alight with passion, the harsh lines eliminated from his smooth olive face. He also looked irresistible.

"Do you still wish to leave me?"

Because she was still very young, and she was frightened by the intensity of her emotions, Rosalie began to cry. Instantly he was on one knee beside her, his arm enfolding her waist, a clean handkerchief wiping her eyes.

"*Mi corazón, mi queridita, mi amante,* why the tears? Can you not understand what has happened to us? We have found that great love upon which you set such value and in which I have never before believed. You should rejoice, not weep."

Against his shoulder, she said forlornly, "We have no future. You must marry money, and I will be no man's mistress."

"Money? Bah! Didn't I say at dinner I am going to sell the Castillo? You like the south, do you not? You would be content to live here in this poor house?" He raised her face from his shoulder, so that he could look into it. "I am not asking you to be my mistress, Rosa, but my wife."

She stared at him incredulously. As he knelt beside her, his eyes were on a level with her own. Some unoccupied part of her brain noted that they were so dark that pupil and iris were one, and they looked like black velvet.

"You . . . you mean it, Rafael?"

"I would not say so if I did not."

"You . . , you love me?"

Fire seemed to kindle in the depths of his eyes, and the arm encircling her squeezed her waist.

"Haven't I demonstrated that I do?" he asked fervently.

"Oh, Rafael!" She wound her arms about his neck, hardly daring to believe that this miracle had happened.

For a fleeting second she saw the familiar satirical smile twist his lips, and she experienced a moment's chill. Then his lips sought hers, and all was forgotten in ecstasy.

They went hand in hand to inform the Condesa of their engagement, Rosalie in a state of trepidation, for surely Doña Teresa would not welcome a dowerless bride? To her surprise, Rafael's mother expressed profound satisfaction.

"You are good girl, Rosa," she told her, "besides being a pretty one. You will make my son a good wife, and you will never let him down."

"That I never will," Rosalie declared fervently.

Both of them were thinking of Consuelo.

When they were alone, the Condesa apologized for purloining Rosalie's portfolio.

"He was hesitating," she explained, "wondering how you felt about him, and I was sure that those so revealing sketches would assure him of his success. When a man has been jilted he needs to be very sure before he ventures a second time."

Rosalie was unaware that she had ever shown those pictures to Doña Teresa, but she supposed she must have, for surely the Condesa would not pry among her private belongings.

"I had no idea that he . . . he felt like that about me," she said childishly. "He has always been so aloof."

"You are very lovable, Rosa," the Condesa said reassuringly. "And naturally Rafael held himself aloof until he was sure of his own feelings, and yours." She looked at the girl curiously. "You think more of his love than having an establishment?"

"But of course," Rosalie exclaimed impetuously. "I'm not mercenary, madam. Love is what is important. Besides . . . " She checked herself. She had not yet told the Santaellas that she was the Rosalie Smith who in a little more than two years' time would come into a fortune. She was thankful that Rafael did not know that; it meant that his love was not motivated by monetary gain. Nor did she mean to disclose her secret just yet. There had been too much talk about fortunes and dowries, subjects she found repugnant. The revelation would be her wedding present to him, who believed she had nothing to give him except herself.

The Condesa did not appear to notice her uncompleted sentence, but exclaimed sententiously, "Ah, how beautiful is young love, and how impractical!

Still, as long as Rafael has Casa Blanca you will have a roof over your heads."

"That's all we'll need," Rosalie assured her.

Being not entirely ignorant of Spanish customs, Rosalie shrank from making their engagement public, for although the Santaellas were a much diminished family, they possessed a horde of distant connections, who would expect to be allowed to offer their felicitations and be given an opportunity to inspect the bride. Rafael could not understand her point of view.

"I wish the whole world to see the beautiful woman who is to be my wife," he told her.

"I shall feel like a specimen under a microscope."

"*Absurdo!*"

"They'll know I'm a foreigner and wonder what you see in me, since they'll believe I'm bringing you nothing."

"*No importa,*" he declared. "You yourself are a gift beyond price."

The assurance was music in her ears, in spite of its exaggeration.

"But there will be criticism and incredulity," she insisted, for she was thinking of Eloisa. "Couldn't we finish the summer here without saying anything? Let it be our secret."

She still could not believe that this imperious man could truly love her. She seemed to be living in a fantasy engendered by the hot golden days, the purple dusks and shining stars. She had an unreasonable fear that if the everyday world were allowed to intrude upon her idyll it would melt away like the gossamer stuff of dreams. But Rafael had no sympathy with fantasies and dreams, his outlook being wholly practical; moreover, her suggestion offended his Spanish sense of propriety with its hint of a clandestine union. It was bad enough that he was living in the same house with her. He even contemplated returning to Las Aguilas until their wedding. His mother approved of that suggestion, but Rosalie was dismayed.

"Why must we accept these stupid conventions?" she asked angrily. "We're happy here, just the three of us." She looked at him doubtfully. "At least I am."

His dark eyes glowed.

"*Queridita,* I have not your cool temperament. Your presence is a daily temptation."

But he said no more about going to the castle.

An added irritant was the frequent visits of the Carvello brother and sister. Eloisa was pursuing Rafael relentlessly and encouraging Luis to pay his attentions to Rosalie. Her feminine intuition told her that she might have a rival in the English girl, though she would never believe that Rafael could have serious intentions in that direction. Rafael did not mind Eloisa's blandishments, for they fed his male ego, but he furiously resented Luis's attentions to Rosalie.

"You're being ridiculously jealous," Rosalie scolded him after one of the Carvellos' visits. "You know you have no cause to be."

"Of course I am jealous of every man who approaches you," he returned. "Would you have it otherwise? No Spanish girl believes a man loves her unless he shows frantic jealousy."

"So it's all an act, like the prescribed formula for lovemaking. But you needn't put it on for me."

"You speak in riddles. I am jealous of every glance you waste upon Carvello."

"Don't you trust me?"

His face darkened. "I have little reason to trust women."

Rosalie knew he was remembering Consuelo. She cried out impulsively, "But she didn't love you, and I do."

Their argument ended in a fond embrace, but she sensed the tension in him and realized something of the strain the situation was inflicting upon him, for he would never dream of consummating his love, before marriage, with the woman he meant to make his wife. But while she was content to wait, his male ardor was aching for fulfilment. The solution would seem to be a speedy wedding, but that the Condesa opposed. The thing must be done properly, she insisted—all the distant relatives invited, no hole-and-corner affair as if the couple had something to be ashamed of. Besides, it would take time to make Las Aguilas ready for the bride and bridegroom.

"But Rafael said he was going to sell it," Rosalie objected. The prospect of a gathering of starchy Spaniards within the forbidding walls of the castle was daunting. "Since we're going to live at the Casa Blanca, can't we be married in Andalusia?"

"It would not be suitable," the Condesa said decidedly. "Nor can Rafael part lightly with his ancestral home. The farm has prospered this year. Perhaps it will not be necessary to dispose of the castle; there will be enough money to do the necessary repairs."

"That would be rather a waste," Rosalie protested, "for I would never want to live there."

The Condesa gave her an enigmatic look.

"A Spanish wife lives where her husband chooses," she told her repressively.

Rosalie said no more, but if Doña Teresa supposed that marriage would make her meek and submissive, she was going to have a few surprises. All the same she felt vaguely disquieted, and she appealed to Rafael the next occasion when she found herself alone with him. That did not often happen, for Doña Teresa took her duties as a chaperone seriously.

"Naturally mama is reluctant to have the Castillo pass to strangers," he told her. "It is a symbol of family prestige to her. But she could not live there alone, so I am afraid she will have to reconcile herself to its disposal."

"She will continue to live with us?" Rosalie asked in dismay.

"But *claro*. Do you expect me to turn her out?"

"No . . . but . . . ." The prospect of her mother-in-law always being there was depressing.

"You may be glad of her help when *los niños* come," Rafael said, and Rosalie blushed. Remembering what the Condesa had said about grandparents, she realized that she would have to make a good many adjustments before she could accept her husband's mode of life.

Rosalie wrote to Philip, giving him her address, and asking for news. It was a preliminary to announcing her engagement. She knew he would be astonished to learn that she was with the Condesa, and possibly not too pleased. Let him absorb that fact before she sprang on him the news that she was about to console the jilted bridegroom. She also made her query about the whereabouts of the diamond bracelet.

Philip replied at once. He was married to Consuelo and Uncle George's initial opposition had been overcome when he discovered his wife had money. He had bought an apartment for them in Paris. "With my money, of course," Philip wrote.

But by calling it an investment of trust funds he

has managed to circumvent the will. It is an investment, for he bought the whole block and draws rent from the other apartments. Con's father is also reconciled now that he knows my prospects and has come up with a handsome allowance, which is merely a foretaste of good things to come. So everything in the garden is blooming, and when you're tired of dancing attendance on that stuffy countess of yours, come and visit us. Con will be delighted to get to know you. As for the bracelet, I suppose Don Rafael put you up to asking about it. He did give it to Con, you know, but the jeweler, Señor Cortez, couldn't give us its true worth. He is therefore holding it in pawn as it were, but Con won't ever want to claim it. She hates the thing. Your loving brother, Phil. P.S. How on earth did you inveigle yourself into the Santaella household? Take care, pet, there seems to be something sinister in the background.

Just how sinister that background had been to begin with, Rosalie would never let Philip know. Rafael had only referred to it once, and then to apologize.

"We Santaellas are a proud, vindictive race," he told her, "and I had been deeply insulted. I misjudged you entirely. I thought you were a scheming little adventuress whom I need not respect."

"When did you change your opinion of me?" she asked, recalling the significance of the *alcoba de felicidad.* Had Rafael really meant to use her as a substitute for Consuelo?

He flushed uncomfortably, "It was mama who pointed out that I was making a mistake. She insisted you were innocent, my sweet, and that I would be acting shamefully by making you a scapegoat for your brother. But I would never have forced you. It never occurred to me that that would be necessary. I was convinced that once your initial indignation had subsided, the genuineness of which I doubted, you would have surrendered."

Women usually entered his house willingly, he had told her cynically a while back. He knew his power to attract them. She supposed there had been a sequence of affairs and repressed a flash of jealousy. She could expect no less, Rafael was past his first youth and a virile man.

"The incident is painful to recall," he went on. "I would ask you to be generous enough to forget it."

"I'm afraid I can't do that," she said smiling.

"Was it so unforgivable?"

"It's not that, but if you hadn't intercepted me, we should never have come to know each other." A spark of mischief lit her gray eyes. "If I had been really plain, would you have been tempted to test my availability?"

"I knew you were *muy hermosa*," he returned. "I saw that when you waited upon me at the table in the hotel." He smiled ruefully.

Rosalie felt a surge of triumph. Even when he had believed that she was a humble waitress and of doubtful reputation, he had been attracted to her, and while he was officially engaged. Thinking of the other girl, she said, "But I can't compare with Consuelo."

"No, you cannot," he returned. "She was unfaithful to her promises. You said you kept yours."

"I do, but I have neither her beauty nor her dowry." She emphasized the last word deliberately. After her experience with Garth she could not hear too often that she was loved for herself alone.

"To me you are far lovelier than she," Rafael said ardently. "I do not care for those dark sultry types, my English Rose."

He returned to the subject of her abduction, which she could see was causing him considerable distress.

"It was unworthy of a Spanish *caballero,*" he told her.

The unwelcome thought flitted through Rosalie's brain that he was less distressed by the way he had treated her than by the tarnished image he now saw of himself. She instantly dismissed the thought as uncalled-for and promised to forgive and forget. But she was well aware that the dark depths she had glimpsed in him then were still present beneath his surface charm and courtesy, and if ever she were foolish enough to offend him, retribution would be swift and merciless. But they loved each other and love would teach forbearance and tolerance, of that she was confident. By exercising tact and consideration she would learn to humor his touchy pride, and if they were fortunate, they would have a mutual bond in their children. She had learned enough of the Spanish mentality, its obsession with the family, to know that though Rafael loved her as a woman, he would venerate her as the mother of his sons.

Then Rafael announced that he must pay a visit to Las Aguilas to see that all was well there, and insisted that upon his return they would fix the date for their marriage and make their engagement public.

"I wish to claim you as my *novia* before all the world," he told Rosalie. "I have humored your bashfulness long enough. Nor can I wait much longer for my bride." His dark eyes were smoldering. "And though I cannot give you the Santaella betrothal bracelet, I will bring back something worthy of you from Madrid."

"Please don't be extravagant," Rosalie besought him, wincing at the reminder of the missing diamonds. "I don't want jewels, Rafael, only your love."

"The one is the token of the other," he told her. "There is no reason why you should not have both."

Except his alleged poverty. Rosalie watched him drive away with a little crease between her brows. Was Casa Blanca really doing so well that such an extravagance could be justified? But there were degrees of poverty, and the Santaellas lived in a style that seemed more like affluence to her, who had had to skimp and save on a cashier's wage. She smiled to herself, hugging her secret knowledge. She too had a gift for her beloved. When Rafael returned she would tell him that far from wedding a dowerless bride, in a couple of years' time she would be bringing him wealth.

CHAPTER SEVEN

THE CASA SEEMED DULL and empty without Rafael's magnetic presence. Rosalie had retrieved her portfolio of drawings, but the Condesa said nothing about the proposed art lessons. Rosalie suspected the whole idea had been part of a scheme to bring Rafael up to the point of proposing to her. Why the Condesa should be so anxious to marry her to her son, she could not imagine, except for a few subtle hints that he had led a somewhat irregular life before he became contracted to Consuelo, and his mother feared he might revert to it. She wanted to see him settled and a family on the way. Her championship of Eloisa had merely been another of her subtle moves. Knowing Rafael disliked the girl, she had sought to drive him in another direction by pointing out the advantages of marrying her, but why she favored Rosalie instead of the well-dowered Eloisa was puzzling, except that she disliked the Carvellos. What had happened to the foreign bride she had sponsored was another conundrum. Rosalie suspected uneasily that she was a pawn in some intricate game Doña Teresa was playing, but where she fitted in she had no idea; she knew now that she had greatly underestimated her employer, but being direct and honest herself, she was contemptuous of her manipulative ways. Intrigue seemed to be the breath of life to Spanish matrons, who had little else to occupy their minds.

On the afternoon after Rafael's departure, the Carvellos arrived, accompanied by their mother. It was just after siesta time when they appeared at the Casa, so they must have cut short their own rest, for the day was still very hot. Blinding sunlight poured down upon the trees and bushes, making the shadows they cast look black.

Eloisa was daringly wearing trousers with a sleeveless top, but her short legs did not look attractive in pants. She was obviously put out to discover Rafael's absence, but Luis was elated. Drinks were brought out to them in the patio, which was in shade, and while Eloisa sulked and the two older women gossiped, Luis, seated beside Rosalie, endeavored to flirt with her. Every glance from his mischievous blue eyes was full of meaning, and his foot sought to press hers beneath the wrought-iron table. Her lack of response seemed to only inflame his ardor. Two days earlier she would not have minded, but now she felt she was being disloyal to her absent lover. Rising from her chair, Rosalie said she had a headache and begged to be excused. Unfortunately Luis took this announcement to be an invitation.

"Let me drive you out to the mountains, where we can find some fresh air," he proposed. "That will soon dispel your headache." He looked at her expectantly.

The Condesa gave him a black look, evidently considering matters were going too far. Before Rosalie could refuse, she said sharply, "*Un momento, por favor.*" She smiled at her companions. "I think we have kept you in the dark too long, *mis amigos*. My son, upon his return, will have an announcement to make, but since you are such close friends, I will tell you in advance."

She paused dramatically, while the three Carvellos stared at her curiously.

Dismayed, Rosalie exclaimed, "Not now, please, madam. Let Rafael tell them."

The Condesa's black eyes glinted. "It must be now, Rosa, before that young man—" she indicated Luis "—puts you and himself in a situation which will offend your *novio*. *Sí, mis amigos,* we are to welcome Rosa Smith into the family. She and Rafael are to be married."

Had she dropped the proverbial bombshell she could not have more startled her audience. Señora Carvello's jaw literally dropped, Luis drew away from Rosalie as if she had become contagious, while Eloisa's face sharpened into furious rage.

"I do not believe it!" she shrilled. "That scheming whey-faced *Inglesa*! Why, he is practically engaged to me."

She sprang to her feet, her fingers curving like claws.

"You know he is not," the Condesa said coolly. "Sit down, Eloisa. There is no reason for you to scream like a fishwife."

Slowly the Spanish girl relaxed. She sat down again as directed while her mother observed, "This is a very great surprise, Condesa, so you must forgive my daughter's outburst. Don Rafael had certainly led her to suppose . . . but *ay di mi,* we know he is fickle, that one." She gave Rosalie a spiteful look. "Señorita Smith has much greater opportunities living in the same house and she has not neglected them. My felicitations, *señorita.*"

Luis was looking at Rosalie reproachfully.

"You might have given me a hint," he complained. "But let me add my congratulations."

The Condesa was smiling serenely, pleased with the consternation her words had caused. She did not like the Carvellos and after today she did not anticipate she would have to entertain them again.

Rosalie thanked them for their good wishes, adding, "But I really do have a headache." She gave the Condesa an appealing look, "So if you will excuse me . . . ."

She felt she could not stay there any longer, the target of Eloisa's malicious glances and Luis's plaintive ones.

"You do look pale," Doña Teresa admitted. "Very well, *chica,* we will permit you to depart. You had better lie down until dinnertime."

Rosalie performed the ritual handshaking that was etiquette among that society, but omitted the kiss on the women's cheeks. That she felt would seem to them like the kiss of Judas. As it was, Eloisa could barely bring herself to touch her fingers, and only Doña Teresa's watchful eye ensured her good manners. Rosalie fled thankfully to the solitude of her room. Why did the Condesa have to announce her engagement when Rafael was not there to support her, she thought stormily. As for Luis Carvello, she could manage him without such a drastic remedy. At least now they would be free of Eloisa's visits, but she had a faint regret for Luis. He was good company and she was sorry if she had hurt him, but she did not think that his fancy went very deep.

She must have fallen asleep, for when she awoke the shadows were beginning to gather. She got up, tidied her dress and did her face and hair. About to step out on to the patio, she halted in surprise, for Señora Carvello was still there. She and the Condesa were sharing a bottle of sherry, from which they obviously had been imbibing freely, for both were a little mellow.

Standing behind a concealing fall of vine, Rosalie hesitated. She did not want to intrude upon the elderly couple who seemed to be enjoying a confidential gossip, and she wondered what had happened to the two young people. She did not wish to encounter them again, either. Suddenly she became aware of what Doña Teresa was saying—she could understand Castilian now after her tuition in the tongue.

"Don Rafael has gone to raise a loan to renovate Las Aguilas. He will have no difficulty in doing that now that he is about to marry money, even though he cannot put his hands upon it until she is twenty-five."

"You are sure of that, Condesa? She does not look like an heiress. Her clothes are very cheap."

"I made sure before I agreed to the engagement. We arranged to have the will inspected at the place in London where wills can be seen. The money will, of course, have to be transferred to Swiss banks before being invested in Spain."

"You have a wonderful business head, Condesa," Señora Carvello said admiringly. "But you are positive she is this Rosalie Smith?"

"By good fortune I saw a photograph of her in an English paper; it was taken at the time of her father's funeral. Both the children were depicted clearly. There was also a long obituary that mentioned their peculiar upbringing. He actually made them work in a shop! I recognized her as soon as she told me her name, and would you believe it, she was masquerading as a maid at the *parador*. My poor boy was greatly incensed, you understand, but I made him behave himself." She chuckled throatily. "It hurt his pride to have to court a *criada*, but with such a fortune to be gained, it was worth having patience and humbling himself."

Rosalie stood as if turned to stone, unable to move, while Doña Teresa's words stabbed her. Her dreams were evaporating, her romance shivering to shreds.

Señora Carvello was saying, "But Don Rafael has always been noted for his taste in women. Consuelo Nuñez was beautiful. I see nothing remarkable about the little *Inglesa* except a good skin. Will he be content to settle down with such a nonentity?"

"*No importa,*" the other returned. "He will, of course ensure that she does her duty in the matter of heirs, and *ninos* will keep her occupied. But he will be free to follow his fancies. She cannot be such a fool as to expect him to be faithful."

Rosalie lifted shaking hands to her burning cheeks; the paralysis that had enchained her limbs was passing, and she was able to creep away to her room. She heard the car return to collect Señora Carvello. Luis had taken his sister home and returned for his mother. Knowing the Condesa would be alone since Rosalie had retired, she had stayed to keep her company. Her tongue loosened by the wine, Doña Teresa had been unable to restrain her confidences. She wanted her guest to understand that far from marrying a penniless English girl, Don Rafael was doing very well for himself. That Rosalie herself was realizing all too bitterly.

Lying on her bed, she reviewed the events leading up to her arrival at the Casa Blanca. Like a film they unrolled themselves with painful clarity illuminated by what she had just heard. She recalled her introduction to the Condesa, Doña Teresa's careful appraisal, her demand for her first name. Believing she had recognized the Pas heiress, she had told her son he must treat her with respect. That accounted for Rafael's changed attitude, and while his mother sought to check her prospects, sending an agent to London to inspect the will, he had held aloof. She remembered how he had spoken of the foreign bride his mother had procured for him and his doubts about her suitability. He had had to overcome considerable reluctance before he could bring himself to propose to her. He had found the pill a little too much to swallow, even though it was gilded, and that was why, before he had asked her to become Doña Teresa's companion, he had told her to go. A battle between his avarice and his desire to retain his freedom would account for his violence upon that occasion. But she had insisted upon delaying her departure, threatening to accuse him of abducting her. Rafael had conquered his aversion and had then come up with the companion proposition that she, poor fool, had accepted so gladly. Avarice had won.

After arriving in Andalusia he still procrastinated, so the wily Condesa had enlisted the Carvellos to unwittingly further her plans. She had shown Rafael that Eloisa was the only alternative to Rosalie, and an even more unattractive one. Luis she had encouraged to make Rafael jealous—not of Rosalie's affections, for he could not care less about those, but if Luis won her heart, he would also win the Pas fortune. Rafael must have pointed out that Rosalie's feelings were in some doubt, and he was sensitive enough to shrink from another rejection, so Doña Teresa had borrowed her portfolio without leave to convince him that she was ready to be won. Those foolish romantic portraits could have only one interpretation, an interpretation she herself had taken a long time to recognize: that she had become besotted with the original. The spur of Luis's rivalry had done the rest. He had seen the possibility of her money passing into other hands and so had found it easy to simulate the passion, in which he was a past master, to bring about her complete surrender.

Always she had been suspicious of the motives of the men who had made advances to her, but because she had been so sure that Rafael did not know of her prospects she had believed his protestations were sincere. She had reckoned without his mother, that scheming, subtle woman so triumphant in her success. Rosalie understood now that purpose behind the Spanish lessons and all the other information that had been imparted to her. She was being groomed to be a Santaella wife.

She shivered as she recalled the Condesa's false amiability and pretended affection. She cared nothing for Rosalie as a person; she was merely a means to an end. Left to himself, Rafael would probably never have gone as far as proposing to her, but his mother had spurred him on, determined to secure the Pas fortune. The poker-faced Doña Teresa, in her black silks and laces, weaving her webs, seemed to Rosalie's excited fancy like a black spider. She had no consideration at all for the English girl's happiness; her role was to be to produce children and turn a blind eye to her husband's infidelities.

Rosalie found it easier to whip up resentment against the woman than the man—she found satisfaction in her spider smile—but when her thoughts turned to Rafael she was aware only of an aching void. Of course she must leave him; she could not let this farce of an engagement continue any longer. Ever since she had discovered Garth's mercenary motives, she had sworn she would never let herself be married for her money and had snubbed any would-be suitors. Now Rafael, whom she had thought loved her for herself alone, had stolen her heart while she was unaware of his real purpose.

Fool, she thought miserably, blind fool. Why else should he want to marry her, a foreigner whom he secretly despised? That she had been so easily gulled by his flowery phrases increased her humiliation. She recalled the little satirical smile she had surprised in the midst of his lovemaking. He had been laughing at her simplicity even while he kissed her.

One of the maids knocked on her door, which had been locked against intrusion. Rosalie called out that she wanted nothing and was nearly asleep and she would not want any dinner. The girl withdrew and she hoped fervently that the Condesa would not come to make further inquiries. She could not face her tonight and the thought of food made her nauseous. Late in the evening there was a gentle tap on the door, but Rosalie made no answer and whoever it was went away satisfied that she slept.

Rosalie did not sleep. Endlessly she reiterated her folly. How could she ever have imagined that a man in the Conde's position would have stooped to her without a very strong inducement? It had never occurred to her that he might know about the Pas fortune, nor had he until his mother put him wise. She had fallen into his arms like a callow teenager, succumbing to his practiced kisses, avidly mopping up his empty phrases. He knew only too well how to awaken a woman's response, and his every move had been calculated.

By morning she had gained command of herself

and, feeling drained of emotion, was conscious of only one desire—to confront Rafael with his duplicity before she left. It might be more dignified to go before he returned, but she could not forgo that satisfaction. The charge of being mercenary would possibly flay his pride, for he did not care for plain speaking. She would give him scorn for scorn, hurt for hurt, by expressing her contempt for him. Then she would go.

She was glad of her morning coffee, but pushed aside the rolls and honey untasted. It only took a short while to pack her belongings. Then white and resolute she went to join the Condesa in the patio, for Rafael was expected back at midday.

The Condesa eyed her commiseratingly.

"You are looking very poorly, *pobrecita*. Perhaps you should see a doctor?"

"I'm perfectly well," Rosalie replied coolly. "Just a touch of migraine, but it has passed."

"Rafael will be greatly concerned to find you looking so pale."

"I don't suppose he'll notice," Rosalie said wearily. "Men never do. He'll be too full of his own concerns."

The loan he was trying to raise to tide him over until he could obtain her money to free Las Aguilas from its embarrassments, she thought.

Doña Teresa was too astute not to realize something had upset her young protégé. She said apologetically, "Perhaps I should not have spoken of your engagement to the Carvellos."

"No, madam, you should not have."

Doña Teresa bit her lip. It was the first time Rosalie had ever criticized her.

"That young man was too forward," she muttered. "Because you are English he forgets his manners."

"And English girls are fair game?" Rosalie suggested bitterly. "You also think we are brash and ill-
behaved. You often laugh at us among yourselves,
don't you, madam?"

The Condesa changed color and Rosalie knew that
her shot had gone home. These insolent Spaniards did
make fun of her countrymen even while they took
their money.

"We, too, have some pride," she went on. "Though
we may not express it in the same way you do."

"*Claro,*" Doña Teresa agreed and relapsed into
silence. She did not know what to make of this cold
aloof girl who seemed to have changed overnight, for
Rosalie had altered during those hours of bitter humiliation. She had said goodbye to her girlhood and had
become an adult.

Don Rafael arrived by midmorning, but only his
mother went to greet him. Hearing the sound of the
car, Rosalie retreated to her room and sat waiting,
absently watching the sunlight filter through the vines
that surrounded her window. Vines grew everywhere
in that part of the country and were used to make the
potent wines of Spain, red and gold like the Spanish
colors. Red also was the passionate blood that ran in
the veins of her sons, men without compromise, cruel
and proud. What tenderness they possessed was
reserved for their own kin, and Rafael had never
shown her any. Spain had proved too strong a draft
for an unsophisticated English girl.

The Condesa knocked upon her door and pushed it
ajar, breaking into her thoughts.

"Rafael is here, Rosa. He is asking for you."

She had expected Rosalie to run to meet him in her
impulsive way, but since she had not, she was wonder-

ing if this puzzling English girl had turned suddenly shy.

But the level gray eyes held no hint of bashfulness, as Rosalie said coolly, "He'll need a wash and a change, to say nothing of a drink, after his hot journey. I'll come to him later."

The Condesa's arched eyebrows rose in alarmed dismay.

"*Chica,* is something wrong? Have you another migraine?"

Rafael called, "Rosa!" and appeared behind his mother. He was, as she had expected, travel stained and dusty, dressed as when she had met him in the road in an open shirt and trousers, with the twist of scarlet scarf at his throat. Dust powdered his hair and arms, but his eyes brightened at the sight of her, and Rosalie's heart gave a lurch.

Sternly repressing the stir in her pulses, she told him, "I will join you in your office in half an hour."

Eager anticipation changed to bewilderment.

"What a cold welcome!" He took a step toward her, while his mother drew back. "Why this sudden formality, *pequeña?*"

"This is my bedroom," she pointed out. "I will say what I have to say in more suitable surroundings."

Mother and son exchanged puzzled glances. The light died out of the Conde's eyes. He stared at Rosalie for a few minutes in silence and unable to bear his close scrutiny, she turned away from him toward the window. The vine leaves made mauve patterns on the white dress she was wearing, and her profile was a carved ivory cameo against their shade. She looked as remote and as unapproachable as a virgin votary of some classic order.

Rafael gave a sharp sigh, shrugged and went out of the room. The Condesa lingered, seemed about to say something, thought better of it and withdrew, closing the door behind her.

Rosalie glanced at her watch, as she had said she would give him half an hour in which to make himself presentable and to digest her cool reception. To fill in the time she fiddled with her hair and retouched her makeup. Normally she used very little, for it was unsuitable amid her rural surroundings, but noticing how pale she was, she applied a blusher to her cheeks.

"War paint," she murmured as she surveyed herself in her mirror.

Her burning resentment at being fooled, her deep hurt needed expression before she could find peace. She could not keep her emotions bottled up inside her to fester concealed. One blazing explosion and then it would all be over. She was that sort of girl. She was too upset to feel any fear of Don Rafael, and he could not wound her more than he had already done.

At the end of the prescribed half hour, she tapped on his office door.

"*Adelante.*"

She had been a little apprehensive that he might attempt a physical demonstration to break down her defenses, though she was determined not to yield to him. One glance at him assured her that such fears were groundless. Her cold greeting had awakened his own pride. He was standing with his back to the window as she went in. He had changed into a formal suit, and his hair still glistened from the washing it had received. His shadowed face was hard as stone.

While she hesitated, wondering how to frame her accusation, he forestalled her by saying coldly, "You have come to tell me that you have changed your mind."

She was taken aback by his calm detachment; she had expected protests, recriminations, anything but this quiet acceptance.

"Yes," she said simply.

"That being so, you will wish to leave."

"At once, if I may," she told him firmly.

He moved to the table and pulled the cashbox that stood upon it toward him.

"Where will you go?"

"To my brother in Paris."

"As might be expected." He unlocked the box. "You will need extra money for your fare—what Señor Gomez gave you will not cover it from here, nor do I wish you to have to endure any discomfort."

This unexpected solicitude nearly unnerved her. It would have been more in character if he had told her to get out as he had done once before without caring where she went or how. But did she know his character? Did it contain unknown facets?

"I'd rather not take anything from you," she murmured.

"Don't be stupid," he told her curtly. "There is no one else to help you and you must go by train. I will not allow you to risk sunstroke trying to travel cheaply on country buses."

"Thank you," she said meekly. "I'll pay it back, every peseta, as soon as I can."

He smiled sardonically. "Always so independent, but a small loan won't break me. You can consider it as wages; you have been paid nothing for your services."

"All the same I would prefer to pay it back."

"As you please." He unlocked the box and began to take some notes out of it.

Unable to believe that he would let her go without some explanation, she blurted out, "Don't you want to know why I . . . I've changed?"

"It is obvious, is it not?" he returned. "Somehow you have discovered that I knew you were the Pas heiress. You believe that I asked you to marry me to gain your fortune. You have convinced yourself that my motives were not love but money, though it is the custom among us for a woman to bring a dowry with her, even when the couple *is* in love." Again his sardonic smile. "So your pride is offended beyond forgiveness. You have decided that I am despicable, is it not so?"

Rosalie nodded miserably, the hot words she had meant to hurl at him dying away unuttered.

"So, since you wish to leave me, I will not try to stop you, *amante.*"

The endearment twisted her heart, but it was only a figure of speech to him. She would not soften, she must not soften.

Desperately she said, "I despise fortune-hunters, Don Rafael, and you're not the first man who has had an eye on my prospects. I should have known that was what drew you to me. It was . . . unlikely . . . that you could really feel anything for Rosalie Smith, poor creature that she is, no blue blood, no dignity. But it hurt me—" her hands flew to her throat "—to discover that your protestations of love were . . . were . . . ." Her voice died away.

"Were what?" he prompted gently.

"An act to gain my . . . acceptance. An act that you've no difficulty in making seem convincing—

you've had so much practice." He uttered an exclamation, but she rushed on unheeding. "I was sure you didn't know about Pas. I thought . . . ."

Her anger had burned away, and she no longer wanted to denounce him. She turned aside to hide the yearning in her eyes. "I believed you loved me," she whispered.

"And now you're convinced I do not?"

"You can't persuade me otherwise."

Yet she looked at him with a glimmer of hope, to find his face inscrutable, his eyes like jet.

"Then I shall not try to delude you further," he said proudly.

"I should hope not," she cried wildly. "I know you're incapable of love; you've always derided it. You care only for stones and mortar, Las Aguilas and your family pride. You're inhuman!" She choked on a sob.

Rafael did not move but continued to regard her stonily; nor did he contradict her. Rosalie was a little surprised by his silence, she had not thought he would relinquish her fortune without making a fight for it, but she did not want any more false protestations and was relieved that he had taken her rejection so quietly.

"I'm afraid you've had a wasted journey," she told him. Contrarily she wanted to sting him into some sort of response, even while she was thankful for his forbearance.

"Why so?"

"Weren't you going to raise a loan to renovate Las Aguilas in view of your, er, improved position?"

"Whoever told you that?" he asked, astonished.

"The Condesa."

"I see." He looked at her enigmatically. "And you believed her? It was what you would expect of me?"

"It was logical. At least *she* is frank."

A spark of anger showed in his eyes.

"And you think I would use your money to save that ruin? That I lied to you when I said I was going to sell it?"

"I wouldn't put it past you."

As soon as the words were out she realized how wounding they must be if he had spoken the truth. But surely he had lied!

"*Mil gracias* for your good opinion," he said sarcastically and turned abruptly to the window, staring out of it. The shadow of the vines fell across his face, accentuating its harsh planes, the bitter twist of his lips. Her heart went out to him in a surge of longing. She wanted to cry out that if he needed her money, he could have every penny of it if he would take her along with it, but prudence restrained her. The Condesa's words returned to her with added force. Having no love for her he would not be faithful, he would desert her for more attractive women, once he was sure of her fortune, perhaps even spend her money upon them. She recalled that she had read somewhere that in Spain a woman could not touch her property without her husband's consent, nor could she even obtain a passport without his concurrence. She had enough of her father's hard-headedness to know that she would be making a very poor bargain. She could not even be sure that she would have children for solace during his neglect. Not that she consciously tabulated these drawbacks during those moments of stress; they were to return to her later. She only knew then that she must not obey the urgency of her heart.

Because she was in pain, she said sweetly, "I'm sure Eloisa Carvello will be only too happy to console you, and she has a not inconsiderable dowry. They always say third time lucky."

He swung around as if she had struck him and strode toward her, a blaze of fury on his face. She did not move and her nerves quivered with anticipation, expecting some sort of physical onslaught. Even in anger she would welcome his arms.

Inches from her he halted, with difficulty restraining himself, and said coldly:

"*Por Dios,* Rosa, you hit hard. There, take the money and be gone before I forget myself."

He again turned his back upon her.

Mechanically Rosalie gathered up the notes, murmuring that she would consider them a loan, and looked uncertainly at his unresponsive shoulders.

"I will arrange for someone to drive you into Cordoba," he said without looking around. "You had better leave at once. There is a train to Madrid this afternoon that you should be able to catch."

"Thank you, *señor.*" She hesitated. "So this is goodbye?"

"*Claro,* you have no wish to prolong this impossible situation."

"Certainly not. *Adiós,* Don Rafael."

He turned around, his face a marble mask.

"*Adiós,* Señorita Smith. A pleasant journey."

She moved slowly toward the door, and he sprang forward to open it for her. She was really leaving, she would never see him again. She passed through with bowed head, aware that tears had started to her eyes, but she must not let him see her weep.

Blinking, she heard him say from behind her, "It is possible, you know, that you may have misjudged me," and heard him shut the door forcibly between them.

CHAPTER EIGHT

ROSALIE DID NOT SEE either the Condesa or her son again. Both were shut away in their rooms when the hired car arrived to take her to Cordoba. From Madrid she flew to Paris and Philip met her at the airport.

"Your wire came as a bit of a surprise," he told her. "We thought you were dug in for the rest of the summer."

Rosalie offered some vague excuse, saying the hot climate had been too much for her. Noting her pale face and ringed eyes, her brother asked no questions. Intuitively he guessed there was a lot more she did not wish to mention and passed on to his own affairs. Con, he said, would be delighted to welcome her and she must make a long stay with them.

Uncle George had been most cooperative. At first deploring Philip's marriage to a Peruvian, whom he half expected to be a sort of gypsy barbarian, he succumbed completely to Consuelo's beauty and feminine charm when he met her. Moreover, her nationality was more than compensated for by her fortune. The apartment block was a way of investing some of the money he held in trust for his nephew, and was in his opinion quite a legitimate transaction. Philip was leased the best apartment within it, for which he paid a nominal rent until the whole building would become his as part of his inheritance.

Rosalie resolutely sought to put Rafael out of her mind, for she had too much to do to spend time pining for a lost idyll. She went to see her mother, and Ma Pas greeted her without much enthusiasm. She was a faded, pretty woman who had come to care for little except her own comfort. She had been entirely dominated by her forceful husband and had meekly submitted to his decrees, including his plans for her children. Like a Spanish wife, Rosalie thought, and like a Spanish widow, the woman had never discarded her mourning black. What little initiative she had possessed had been crushed by Philip Alexander, and now that he had gone she merely drifted. *Would I have become like that,* Rosalie wondered, *if I had married Rafael?* But she had much more character than her mother, who admired her independent spirit but was secretly a little afraid of her. She was too much like her father. What affection Mrs. Smith was capable of she lavished on her son.

Señor Nuñez still lingered in Paris, for Consuelo was expecting, and he did not want to return home until after the birth of his grandchild. Inevitably Rosalie met him at Consuelo's home, but though he looked at her rather oddly, he never mentioned the Santaellas. Though regretful of the Smiths' lack of pedigree—a supermarket was not as distinguished as a *castillo*—he appreciated Philip's prospects and was moved by his daughter's radiant happiness. Since Uncle George still held the purse strings he saw to it that there was no lack of money in the Parisian household, and Philip was able to give time to his desire to write.

Both insisted that Rosalie should make her home with them, but she was unwilling to intrude upon their bliss. There was an attic at the top of the block and she

asked if she might rent it and manage for herself. It
had a north light and would make an excellent studio.

"It is not necessary that you should do that," Consuelo demurred, having all the Latin's regard for family. "You are my Felipe's twin sister and all that we
have is yours to share."

Rosalie thanked her, but insisted upon having sepa-
rate quarters.

"You'll see more than enough of me," she told her
sister-in-law. "I'll be dropping in whenever I feel lonely, and when the baby comes I'll be glad to help in any
way I can."

She had come back from Spain no longer the impulsive girl who had taken the job at the Hotel Marqués
de Valpenza as an adventure and means of escape
from an uncongenial life at Pas. She was a woman,
who intended to control her own destiny and direct it
in the way she wished to go. She had finished with love
and romance and meant to concentrate all her ener-
gies on her art.

She was accepted as a student in a famous atelier.
The maestro, a well-known artist, took one look at her
Spanish sketches and enrolled her among his pupils on
the spot. But before she could settle down to work, she
had to go to London to tackle Uncle George.

As she walked through the familiar streets and
passed the glittering facade of a Pas store with its gar-
ish labels advertising reductions and "good buys" she
felt as though a whole century of experience, instead
of little more than six months, lay between her and the
girl who had worked there at a cash desk. As she
looked up at it she formed another resolution. The
love of money was the root of all evil; money had
deprived her of true happiness. She did not want the

fortune that was coming to her; it should be bestowed elsewhere. She watched the busy shoppers pouring in and out of the glass doors. This was Philip Alexander's legacy to posterity, but hers should be something very different. He had found fulfillment in the erection of these monstrosities of glass and steel, but hers lay in a totally different direction, and she had as much right to fulfill herself as her father had. So she told Uncle George.

"I can't afford to wait until I come into my money," she said, "to waste another two years. I need training now. You got around the will in Philip's favor by calling his home an investment. Surely you can invest in my talent."

"Much too risky," he said, shaking his gray head. "You'd much better go back to your cashier's cage, my dear, and in two years' time you may have forgotten this nonsense. I know something about the *vie de bohême*. Artist is another name for layabout."

"Don't show your ignorance," she snapped. "A famous artist has assessed my work and is ready to teach me. He's choosy about his pupils, I can tell you. You're correct when you speak of a cashier's cage, but you'll never cage me again."

George was secretly a little overawed by this cool, determined young woman. She had changed very much since he had last seen her, and she had improved. The gaucherie of youth had been ironed away, her face showed more character and she was beautiful. He realized the last fact with surprise. Rosalie had always been a pretty girl, but he had not appreciated the symmetry of her clear-cut features, the loveliness of her large gray eyes. Her hair had grown longer and she wore it swathed around her head,

showing the graceful curve of her neck. Old Philip's
daughter had turned out a beauty—well, well. She
would be wasted in a store.

"Your father left his money as he did because he
didn't want it thrown away upon senseless
extravagancies," he pointed out. "Which is just what
you want to do."

"I won't be extravagant, uncle, and I shall have to
work very hard to make up for lost time. I require only
a small allowance to keep me until I can earn for
myself. If I can't make a go of it, I'll do something else,
but I'm confident I shall. I'll never go back to Pas. If
you don't want to use the trust money, you could quite
well afford to make me a loan and charge me interest.
I'll repay you when I'm twenty-five. And that's
another thing—I don't want all that wealth. I shall
give it to charity."

Uncle George threw up his hands. "Now surely
you're mad!"

"Not at all. A lot of money can be a curse. Even the
prospect of it has caused me great unhappiness. The
possession would only make me miserable," she said
bitterly. "At least if I'm poor, I shall know what
friends I make are genuine and not seeking to sponge
off my bounty."

And lovers who wooed her for her fortune.

In the end she had her way, her uncle becoming
convinced of her sincerity, the more so because the
sum she requested was so modest. She only needed
food and the minimum of clothing, and, more expensive, her materials. Philip's attic rent was nominal.

The other matter was more difficult of
accomplishment—the return of the diamond bracelet.
Passing through Madrid on her way home she had

called at the jeweller's and ascertained that it was still unsold. Its purchase, too, was to come out of her money, but she could not pretend it was an investment, since she had set her heart upon its return to the Conde.

"To sell it was dishonest," she insisted. "Of course Philip needed the money. Father's will was not a good one, uncle, and it paved the way for such temptations. But it's a slur upon our good name. The Conde is not well off and can't afford such a loss."

The argument continued during the dinner to which George invited her. He was not too old to like being seen out with a beautiful woman and his niece had the advantage of being a perfectly legitimate exhibit. At length, mellowed by wine and good food, gratified by the admiring glances thrown in Rosalie's direction, he capitulated.

"Since you seem to regard the restoration of this trinket of such importance, I'll see it's done, if you tell me where to send it," he promised, "though Philip's peccadilloes are no liability of yours or mine. Still, he has made a good marriage and I've no wish that he should be under an obligation to this Spaniard, who may feel he has a grudge against him, as Connie was once engaged to him. Funny custom, giving a girl a bracelet instead of a nice half hoop of jewels in a ring. Your aunt's was emeralds set in brilliants—we chose it together." He began to wax sentimental over his after-dinner brandy. "Yes, I would be very indignant if she pawned it."

The illustration was hardly appropriate as her aunt had not jilted him, but Rosalie felt elated by her victory. Ever since she had learned of her brother's action she had been determined to return the betrothal bracelet to Don Rafael, though Philip had no qualms about it at all. Now perhaps the Conde would not think so badly of the Smith family. She pictured his astonishment when he opened the packet, but that recalled his dark aristocratic features too vividly for her comfort and she dismissed the mental picture.

Her uncle noticed her pensive look.

"I hope you didn't form any attachment while you were in foreign parts," he said. "Connie's all right, and very nice to look at, but one foreigner in the family's quite enough. It's different when it's the other way around. These Latin types look very romantic, but they're devils to live with."

"I'm sure you're quite right, uncle," she agreed demurely. "But when I was in Spain I was too busy to bother with romance." *God forgive me for that lie,* she thought, but it would never do if she wanted the bracelet returned to let Uncle George discover that she had a personal interest in the recipient. "I shall never marry," she went on. "I'm dedicated to my career."

"I've heard that one before," he told her. "But if men have any eyes in their heads they won't let you be dedicated long. I wish your father could see you now. He'd be proud of you."

"Thank you, uncle, but I doubt it. He took no interest in anything that wasn't directly connected with Pas, and that I don't intend to be any longer."

"You'll change your mind when you're due to get your cut. You won't really give it all away?"

"Oh, but I shall."

"We'll see." He raised his glass. "Here's to my pretty niece who's managed to bamboozle her old uncle very cleverly, and to her success in the mode of life she has chosen."

She again thanked him, smiling at him. She had never liked him so well until that moment, but her heart was aching under the smart silk blouse Consuelo had given her. Consuelo gave her many presents, and she would have to curb her generosity, for she did not want to seem always a taker, never a giver. There would have been no need for such concentration on her work if her connection with a certain Spanish Conde had not been broken. For the hundredth time she pondered over his last words.

"It is possible, you know, that you may have mis-judged me."

Over the money? About his feelings for her? He had given her no chance to ask for an explanation, shutting his door behind her, dismissing her without attempting to defend himself, accepting her departure without protest or question. He could not have loved her at all to have acted so. Or had he taken refuge behind his façade of insolent pride, which would not allow him to stoop to bandy words with her? She would never know. She was as completely severed from him as if he were dead.

So Rosalie went to live under the pantiles of her brother's apartment building and absorbed herself in her work. Her days were spent between the classes at the atelier and her own studio. Occasionally she joined her fellow students in cheap cafés and drank coffee or *vin ordinaire.* She found their discussions stimulating. But when they started on politics, she went home. For her, politics had nothing to do with art.

She had to resist Philip and Consuelo's many invita-tions to go out with them and her sister-in-law's desire to make her attic quarters luxurious.

"Talent thrives on self-denial," she told her. "Many

of the world's masterpieces were created near the breadline. If I grew fat and sleek I couldn't paint."

Words incomprehensible to Consuelo, who had never gone short of anything in her life.

"Ros is a bit mad," Philip told his wife, "but she's a genius. All geniuses are mad. Fame is the spur and all that. She'll be famous one day and then perhaps she'll let you coddle her. I only wish I had half her talent."

For Philip was finding that the road of the would-be author is strewn with rejection slips.

In due course Consuelo's baby was born, a fine healthy boy. They named him after his grandsire, Felipe Alexander, the Spanish spelling being a concession to his mother, but Alex, as they called him, was all Smith.

"He looks more like your child than mine," Consuelo told Rosalie, with faint jealousy.

"He takes after his dad," Rosalie pointed out.

"*Bien,* I cannot have too much of my two Felipes," Consuelo declared.

Rosalie looked down at the fair-skinned baby, a baby with his own looks, not really those of her brother but Philip Alexander. If she had had a son he would have been dark—of that she was certain. The Santaella blood would have predominated. The Condesa had been so anxious that Rafael should produce an heir. By now he had possibly done so. Who had superseded her, she wondered. Eloisa Carvello? She would have been at hand, eager to console the Conde for his second disappointment. Most likely he had wedded her, Rosalie thought disconsolately, and the proud father would bestow what love he was capable of upon his children, love that he could not give to a woman. Rosalie sighed and went back to her painting.

Time passed quickly, the chestnuts in the Champs Elysées budded, bloomed, bore fruit and shed their leaves, until another spring woke them to new life. Alex thrived, learned to sit up, to crawl, and began to cut his teeth. Rosalie drew and painted him, to his mother's gratification. He remained fair, much more like his aunt than Consuelo, but then Rosalie was so like her brother.

Double events appeared on the horizon, the coming of age of the Pas twins and Rosalie's first exhibition. For the former Philip was planning an enormous party, in which Rosalie showed no more than polite interest. She remained steadfast in her determination to dispose of her share of the money, and instructed Uncle George to select those charities he considered most worthy of her behests, a task he did not appreciate. Her exhibition, which came before her birthday, was an event of much greater significance to her.

It opened on a bright spring day. Rosalie stood in a corner of the small gallery watching the people pass, and noting their reactions to what they saw. Her finest picture was called, *The Dispossessed*. Acclaimed an original work of great promise, it had excited controversy and criticism in the press, but also some praise. It therefore rated a visit, but the uninitiated among the visitors did not know what to make of it. They paused, stared and moved away, some of them with puzzled expressions. It had taken Rosalie some months to paint, but its inspiration had been born in Andalusia.

She was sharing the gallery with a fellow artist. Jean Duprez was established, but he admired the girl's work to the extent of offering her to show her pictures alongside his. She had been pleased and flattered, though it had occurred to her he could not regard her as a serious rival if he were so complacent. But once the pictures were hung, she saw that her stark forceful style complemented his futuristic impressions, the heterogeneous splashes of vivid color in peculiar shapes, which was his form of expression, contrasting with the somber blacks, browns and yellows, relieved by occasional vivid scarlet, that distinguished her own efforts.

"At least Ros's pictures have some form," Philip had remarked when he came to the preview. "You can see what they're meant to be, but I'm darned if I know what Duprez is getting at."

"Expressions of moods," Rosalie explained, grinning mischievously. "That purple and emerald study portrays his emotion when confronted with the beautiful nude which you can just discern in the top left-hand corner, though why he sees her with all her anatomy distorted I couldn't tell you. But he sells." She sighed.

"And so will you when you're better known," Philip assured her. "You have a haunting power." He stared at *The Dispossessed*. "I see Spain in that picture of yours and the figure is reminiscent of our mutual pal at Las Aguilas. You didn't waste your time, Ros, while you were there."

The Dispossessed did in fact portray Don Rafael's features against a background of crumbling towers and murky sky. The man's face was arresting in its sad resignation, the acceptance that a golden age had passed, leaving him faced with ruin and desolation. His garb was nondescript, fading into shadow, but his head and face were clear against a break in the heavy clouds, ivory with ebony hair and hopeless eyes. Melancholy was the keynote of the painting, a nostalgia for what had been and would never be again.

Consuelo had said, "I do not like it. It is too sad, and it reminds me of what I want to forget."

She was delighted that some of Rosalie's baby studies were shown.

"Nothing can ever be really forgotten," Rosalie had told her, "and the artist creates from his or her experiences."

Don Rafael's image was still as vivid in her mind as when she had parted from him. She had thought that when she had painted *The Dispossessed* she would get him out of her system, but she had only perpetuated his memory.

Her other canvases were also of Spain, enlargements of the sketches she had done at the Casa, and though the public was dubious, the critics were kind. She had a long way to go, but she showed immense promise.

As might be expected, the more conventional studies she had made of Baby Alex were more popular. In them her vigorous drawing was muted. The one of him, wide-eyed, staring into space, held the essence of a baby's wonder as he becomes aware of the incredible world surrounding him.

While Rosalie effaced herself in her corner, Duprez was doing the honors, a flamboyant figure, red-bearded in an artist's beret and smock. He was a bit of a poseur, but Paris loved him. He was such a character, that *incroyable* Jean, so rude and audacious, but such fun. His fans flooded the exhibition to gape at his incredible pictures, but they saw Rosalie's as well.

Duprez had worked in the same *atelier* with Rosalie, and he had bullied and patronized her. She never minded his outspoken, often cruel criticisms and fenced gaily with his outrageous suggestions, for Jean Duprez was also very amorous.

"You are the only woman who has resisted me," he told her once.

"About time one did," she retorted. "It's no use, Jean. I like you immensely, but I will never sleep with you."

"You are hard-hearted, an icicle; too, too cruel."

"Cruel to be kind. Come off it, Jean. You know it would be a mistake. You and I get on much better on a platonic basis."

He laughed and admitted that she was possibly right.

"But one day you will love," he prophesied. "And it will be devastating. Me, I shall be amused to watch the deluge."

"You'll wait a long time to see that spectacle," she told him. "I have no heart."

She had loved, but that part of her was dead and would never be resurrected.

Rosalie was inconspicuous in her corner, in wide-bottomed black pants and black sweater, thinly embroidered with gold. Slight and boyish, she looked little more than a teenager until the observer met her eyes. Clear and candid, they held knowledge of suffering and resolution to conquer pain. The eyes of a woman who had lived.

As she idly watched the fluctuating crowd, she suddenly caught her breath and stiffened. A man was sauntering through the medley, his uncovered dark head held proudly on arrogant shoulders, a little supercilious smile twisting his thin satirical mouth. Dressed in a dark suit, he looked distinguished . . . and foreign. She did not need the slight stir beside her to tell her who he was.

A smart-looking woman whispered, "The Conde de

las Aguilas. I met him in Madrid. Who would ever have thought to encounter him here?"

She moved as if she meant to make herself known to him, but her companion, a man, restrained her.

"*Tais-toi*. Monsieur le Comte has brought his own diversion."

Beside Rafael tripped a fair woman, wearing a designer dress. She looked a mere girl except for her blasé air, which betrayed experience. She was pretty and petulant. Jean hurried to greet them—evidently he knew the woman—and she introduced him to her escort. Both men bowed. The girl became engaged in lively banter with the artist. Rafael gave them a bored smile and with a faint shrug of his shoulders left them to it, continuing his progress through the room. He stopped before *The Dispossessed*. Then he looked around and saw Rosalie. Almost imperceptibly he beckoned to her and as if drawn by a magnetic force she could not resist, Rosalie went to stand beside him. The years seemed to roll away, they were back in the Casa Blanca and he was looking at her sketches.

"However did you find your way here?" she asked.

"I came because I saw your name advertised," he said simply. "My congratulations, Rosa. You are a great artist."

"Thank you very much, *señor*," she said stiltedly.

It was all over, what had once been between them. He had come out of idle curiosity with the woman of the moment to see what she had done with her talent. Now she could meet him upon neutral ground without emotional complications. She felt very sure of herself and ready to accept his challenge. She wondered what he made of her picture, for which he had been the inspiration.

Together they looked at the proud, defeated face so like his own, and he told her, "That is a wonderful picture, Rosa. It expresses so much with so little—the passing of an era, an era that was gracious and elegant and when men respected their traditions. Oh, you need not tell me that we have created a much better world, where the poor and oppressed have come into their own, but we have also lost our ideals, our values are changed and our sights are lowered. It is a very remarkable picture for a woman to have painted, so strong and stark . . . but then you are an uncompromising individual, are you not, Rosa *mia,* with a backbone of steel."

"That's hardly complimentary," she said, laughing, for though he was praising her as an artist, he was diminishing her as a woman. Spanish women were essentially feminine, and he was telling her she had a masculine talent.

"It was meant to be," he said gravely. "You have become very beautiful, Rosa. Does that please you better?"

She shook her head. "I never cared for compliments on my looks. They're so unimportant."

"What an odd thing to say. I see you are still a prickly pear. Do you remember the prickly pear hedges in Andalusia?" Rosalie bit her lip and turned her head away. Remember? She could never forget.

"Will you dine with me?" he went on. "Or are you so full of engagements you have no time to spare for an old friend?"

The invitation surprised and delighted her. She discovered that she very much wanted to see more of him, if only to show him how indifferent she had become.

"I don't go out much, Don Rafael," she told him. "But I'd be pleased to accept your invitation. But what about the lady you are escorting? Hasn't she first claim on your time?"

A foolish question, even an impertinent one, for obviously if he had asked her out he could not be engaged with the other woman.

He smiled. "I see you are still feminine at heart," he observed and glanced carelessly at the golden head visible across the room. "She is a mere casual acquaintance." He sighed and added, "Man was not intended to live alone, Rosa."

"You're not married, then?"

A shadow crossed his face. "My efforts in that direction have not been very successful." He glanced at her hands. "You are not married, either?"

"No. As I once told you, I'm wedded to my paintbrush. To have achieved all this in under three years has left no time for other interests."

"You must have worked very hard."

She said succinctly, "I have."

"And you have won success."

"Barely, for this is only the beginning. I've a long way to go, Don Rafael, and a great deal more to learn before I consider myself an artist."

"Hm, still dedicated." He looked at her keenly. "Does it satisfy you, or is it second best?"

His perspicacity disconcerted her. Her art had been second best, but now it had become predominant.

"It satisfies me," she said coolly and fleetingly thought of Consuelo's baby. She added, "Any woman can marry and have a child."

"But only Rosa Smith could paint *The Dispossessed*," he agreed. "And that gives you fulfillment?"

She shied away from the implication. "I really don't see how it concerns you," she murmured.

"Don't be prickly. I am merely interested in what makes you tick. You see, I am unfamiliar with the career woman. She is a new phenomenon in my experience."

"It is fulfillment of a very early ambition," she told him. "I always had an urge to paint, but it was suppressed. In a sense you are responsible for its release." He raised his brows, and she went on hurriedly. "When I came back from Spain I was determined that family opposition should no longer stop me. The work I did in your country convinced a great teacher of my potential. So I had my way."

Her voice became flat. She had won a victory over Uncle George, but she had also suffered a defeat. Her unrequited love for the man beside her had contributed to her development, but the process had been painful.

"So now you have all you can desire—success, fulfillment, and you are about to receive your share of the great Pas fortune. You are a fortunate woman, Rosa."

Sudden suspicion darted into her mind. His coming was well-timed. Had he meant to sound her out, discover if she still cherished any tender feelings toward him and make another effort to secure her thousands?

"You've a good head for dates," she told him scornfully.

"Nobody in Paris could fail to learn of the great preparations for the Pas twins' coming of age," he returned. "It's the main topic of the city's gossip."

"Then it may interest you to know that I've renounced my share. It's to go to charity."

She watched him closely for any sign of disappointment, but all she could discern was a faint surprise and a gleam, almost like triumph, in his eyes.

"Now why did you do that?" he asked.

"I don't need it. Others do."

"I never suspected you were a philanthropist."

"It isn't that at all. That beastly money has poisoned every human contact I've tried to make," she cried passionately. People in the crowd were looking at them curiously, and lowering her voice, she asked, "Does our dinner date still stand?"

For a second her implication did not reach him, and then his eyes blazed.

"That was damnable, Rosa, but then your assumptions regarding myself have always been ill-judged."

"Then it's off?" she asked, aware of an acute sense of deprivation.

"By no means." He glanced toward his blonde, who was making her way toward them. "I am feeling a need for more astringent company than pretty kittens. I am sure you will provide it, if you will so honor me."

"I shall endeavor to do so."

He arranged to call for her on the following evening.

"But I would prefer not to meet your brother and his wife, for obvious reasons," he told her. "You live with them, do you not?"

He seemed to have checked up upon her very thoroughly. She explained that she had her own premises.

"Oh, can't you forget the past?" she added impatiently.

"No, that is impossible," he returned ambiguously.

Implacable Spaniard, she thought with irritation, as the blonde reached them. She was introduced as Mademoiselle Lucille Lenoir and was, she told them, a cabaret performer at the Café Royale, and that, Rosalie thought, explained her. Fifty years ago a man like Rafael would not have dared to introduce her, but times changed, and after all, he probably thought there was little to choose between a painter and a dancer. She had no evidence that Rafael's relationship with her was other than it should be, but she was in a mood to decry him, to counteract the upsurge of her old feeling for him that was beginning to destroy her detachment.

Jean joined them.

"You are from Spain, *monsieur,*" he said to Rafael, "and that, no doubt, is why you are so interested in Rosa's work. *Mon ange,*" he turned to her, "you are neglecting me entirely."

"On the contrary, you have been absorbed in entertaining your VIPs," she returned, wondering why he had had to butt in at such an inopportune moment. Rafael was eyeing him with suspicion and distrust.

"Monsieur Duprez is a good friend and a fellow artist," she told him, "but that is all."

"Had I my way there would be a great deal more," Jean announced, leering at her.

"He doesn't mean anything," Rosalie sought to assure Rafael. "He's an incorrigible flirt."

"*Chérie,* must you seek to deflate me in front of *ce monsieur-là?*" Jean inquired reproachfully. "They do not understand *l'amour* in Spain as we do in Paris."

"I hope I have not misunderstood you," Rafael told him coldly. "*Adiós, monsieur.*" He made a slight bow and turned to Rosalie, giving her his brilliant smile. "*Hasta la vista,* Rosa."

He walked away with Lucille in tow toward the exit. Jean watched him go, his red beard bristling.

"The arrogant Spaniard!" he muttered. Then he

laughed. "Give him a cloak, guitar and a rose behind his ear, and that one could make a nun forget her vows. Ever heard of Don Juan, *ma mie?*"

"I believe I have heard him mentioned," Rosalie returned lightly. "What's the connection?"

"*Alors,* that one is another of the same breed, so be warned, *chérie.*"

Then he left her, to mingle with his admirers.

Rosalie remained alone standing in front of *The Dispossessed.* She studied anew the so familiar features. It had taken only one brief encounter to show her that her indifference was a mere pretense and her love for Rafael was far from dead. One glance from those velvet eyes, one glimpse of his charming smile, and it had risen to submerge her. As for him, he had shown no resentment of the past, and had asked her to dine with him, without appearing to be unduly put out when she had told him she had renounced her fortune. New hope was struggling to be born, and it would be too bad if that blundering ass Jean Duprez had spoiled her chances.

CHAPTER NINE

ROSALIE DRESSED with special care for her dinner with Rafael. She was anxious to avoid any suggestion of a Bohemian artist. Consuelo had at an earlier date pressed upon her a black dress that she had declared she had grown too stout to wear, and she was sure with a little alteration it would fit Rosalie perfectly. Rosalie had accepted it with reluctance, observing that she would never have occasion to wear a haute couture gown, for that was what it was, but Consuelo would not be denied.

Fortunately she had taken it in under her sister-in-law's supervision, who had said, "You never know. The occasion may come, how do you say, out of the blue, and you find you have nothing to wear."

And now it had fallen out of the blue and she was grateful for Consuelo's foresight. The dress was made of crêpe with a draped bodice and short sleeves, the skirt falling in graceful folds to the floor from a black and gold brocade sash. Rosalie saw with pleasure that it made her look slim and sophisticated. Rafael had never seen her in a good dress, nor a long one, only in the off-the-rack suits and little cheap dresses she had taken with her to Spain, and Rosalie was a woman who repaid good dressing.

She had her hair done in the morning—an unusual luxury; the hairdresser styled her coiffure with soft waves falling on each side of her face and shaped to

her head. She possessed no jewels, only a necklace of
garnets set in imitation gold, but it was pretty and
complemented her dress. As she slipped on the gilt
chain bracelet that held her watch, she thought of the
diamond one Consuelo had once worn. Rafael must
have received it, for Uncle George had told her he
held his receipt for it. She wondered if he would mention it. She did not mean to betray ever that she, not
Philip, had arranged for its return.

She descended to the vestibule in good time, surmis-
ing that Rafael would come in a taxi, and it would cost
francs to keep it waiting. She had grown up with such
small economies always in mind and thought of them
automatically.

The old man who acted as concierge wished her
good evening and, being a Frenchman, appraised her
with a critical eye. It was not often that Mademoiselle
Smith made a toilette and he obviously approved of
the result.

Rafael arrived punctually, looking distinguished in a
black dinner jacket of more modern style than the
white one he had worn at the *parador*. He carried a
spray of orchids. Seeing him so dear and so familiar,
Rosalie had to check an impulse to run into his arms.
Apparently he half expected her to do so, for he lifted
his arms to receive her; then mindful of the flowers
and the watchful eyes of the concierge, he dropped
them and bowed ceremoniously.

"*Buenos días,* Rosa."

"Shouldn't it be good evening?" she asked archly.

"The evening is still the day." He held out the
orchids. "These would look beautiful on your dress."

She smiled up into his dark face.

"Pin them on me."

He came very close to her to fasten the flowers to the shoulder of her gown. She stood perfectly still under his fingers, which she noticed were unsteady. He swore beneath his breath as he pricked himself with the pin, and with an effort controlled their fumbling. Rosalie's eyes were dancing with triumph, for he was not indifferent. He was excited by her proximity.

The flowers in place, he offered her his arm and they went out into the scented Parisian night, where the spring blossoms on the trees overcame with their perfume the odors of cars and humanity.

"I have reserved a table at the Tour d'Argent," he told her when they were seated in the taxi. "Is that to your liking?"

"Isn't it a bit expensive?" she asked anxiously, for she did not want him to waste his money upon her. "I'd be quite content with a Left Bank café."

"You are not dressed for a café," he told her, " and this is an occasion, Rosa. I am not quite a pauper, you know. My estate prospers."

Sensing that her good intentions had been a little tactless, she hurriedly changed the subject.

"You didn't say what had brought you to Paris. You rarely come to France, do you?"

"No, but on this occasion I had business to transact that required my presence," he told her with slight hauteur.

Rosalie wondered if she had blundered again. The business might be no more than a pursuit of Lucille Lenoir, which would account for his hauteur. From his tone she deduced he resented her innocent question.

They reached the restaurant and she went inside feeling a little dashed. She was expecting so much from this evening, and already there seemed to be constraint between them.

Their table was set in front of a large window through which were visible the towers of Notre Dame across the river. Saying he would order for her, Rafael selected the most expensive dishes on the menu and a sparkling wine of exhorbitant price. Glancing at her with challenge in his dark eyes, he told her, "I refuse to economize tonight."

"If you say so, Don Rafael, but might I inquire if you are trying to ruin yourself, and the prices here are ruinous, to prove something?"

"It is not every night that I have the privilege of entertaining the Pas heiress. Where does the red-bearded one take you?"

"Do you mean Jean Duprez?" She laughed. "Jean doesn't take me anywhere, Don Rafael. The nearest we get to a meal out is bread and cheese and a bottle of *vin ordinaire* in the studio."

"His studio, or yours?"

Jean had never been in her attic, nor would she go out with him alone. What she was referring to were impromptu parties with several of them together.

Unable to resist stirring Rafael's jealousy, for she hoped that was what had prompted the question, she dimpled and told him, "Both."

He looked disapproving and muttered something about loose Bohemian ways, and abruptly she asked about the Condesa.

"She has gone to live with cousins in Madrid," he informed her. "She finds city life more congenial in her declining years."

"Las Aguilas was a bit isolated."

"Las Aguilas is sold and halfway toward being a rival to the Parador de Valpenza," he told her tersely.

"But you said—"

"A lot of foolish things," he interrupted, smiling ruefully. "Pride must give way to necessity. I have invested the proceeds in more land in Andalusia; with them and the sale of the diamonds . . . ." He looked at her sharply. "You know your brother sent the bracelet back to me?"

"I'm glad of that," she exclaimed. "But did you have to sell it? I mean, shouldn't it have been kept for the next Santaella bride?"

"It was too old-fashioned for modern taste," he returned curtly. "Possibly she would prefer a ring."

Rosalie eyed him anxiously, wondering if he had someone in mind, but he was not looking at her. Instead he was concentrating on his plate, devoting all his attention to his food. His long lashes made inky crescents on his olive cheeks, from which he had shaved his sideburns. The light from the rose-shaded lamp on their table softened the contours of his face, making it appear more youthful, but she noticed that there were silver hairs at his temples that had not been there before. He looked more than ever like a Spanish grandee, and was the most distinguished-looking man in the restaurant.

About to tell him that Philip had a son, Rosalie checked herself. Although he believed that her brother had returned the bracelet he had not wanted to meet him, so perhaps the subject of her relative was best avoided. Instead she inquired about the Carvellos. Though he had not yet married Eloisa, they might be engaged. But Señorita Carvello, it transpired, had married a wine exporter in Jerez and Luis was engaged to a local girl.

"I rarely see them," he said. "We were not really compatible."

Rosalie felt a little worry for Eloisa, so much effort to so little purpose, and here she was dismissed as not being compatible.

"So if your mother is living in Madrid, you are all alone at the Casa Blanca?" she asked.

"Yes. But I am much occupied. As I was saying, with the money from the Castillo and the bracelet I have increased my holding. I am breeding horses and black bulls."

"Not . . . not bulls for the bullring?"

"Most assuredly for the *corrida*." Again his eyes challenged her. "We Spaniards are very cruel, you know."

"Only in some ways," she murmured distressfully.

He laughed. "Don't look so upset, *pequeña,* not many of my bulls find their way into the ring—it is not a spectacle I take any pleasure in; it is the tourist interest that keeps it alive."

"I don't believe you're cruel."

"Not when I threatened to put chains on you?"

"You were under a misapprehension," she said, quick to defend him.

His eyes glinted. "Maybe, but there are still times when I would like to do so, though the shackles would not be of iron."

This ambiguous remark seemed to be tending in the direction to which she wanted to lead him, but the waiter intervened with their dessert course, and when he had gone, Rafael said no more on that subject, but began to make some distasteful comments upon the very peculiar appearance of some of the other diners, whose trendy clothes did not meet with his approval.

Desiring to get the conversation back onto a more personal basis, Rosalie asked, "Are you never lonely, or do horses and cattle suffice?"

"They compensate," he returned.

"Do you need compensation, Don Rafael?" she asked provocatively.

He raised his eyes to hers with a depth of meaning in their velvet depths.

"Sí, Rosa," he said softly.

She in her turn looked down at her plate.

"I meant it when I told you my share of my father's fortune is to be bestowed elsewhere," she said quietly. "I shall not go back upon my decision."

"Would it surprise you if I tell you that what you do with your fortune is of no interest to me whatever?"

She looked up quickly to meet his satirical regard, and knew he had guessed the thought that had prompted her statement. She fidgeted with her bread roll, tempted to ask if he had another moneyed girl in view, but knew the question would be unpardonable.

"But you'd expect the girl you marry to have a dowry?" she murmured, then blushed, for her question suggested that she was considering herself as a candidate for that position.

"Not necessarily. I am doing well with my horses and herds." He regarded her intently. "You are obsessed by your inheritance, are you not? You hope by giving it away to free yourself from an encumbrance."

"That's what it seems to me, and it isn't only me who has been obsessed by it."

"That I can believe, but please do not include me among the obsessionists." He drained his glass and set it down deliberately. "It was not your money I wanted, Rosa," he said quietly. "It was because of it that I let you go. Contrary to what you supposed, I am not mercenary. It was your persistence in thinking that I was that so offended me."

"To such an extent that you wouldn't say a word in your own defense?"

The hovering waiter hastened to refill his glass. They both watched the golden liquid flowing from the bottle. Then as the man drew back, Rafael lifted his head proudly.

"The Condes of Las Aguilas do not deign to defend themselves, except with a sword, and you are a woman." He smiled wryly. "Besides, it would not have been any use. I could see you were determined to upbraid me. I could not bear to bandy words with you. Words spoken in anger can inflict wounds that take long to heal."

She wished she could believe him. *Money poisons everything*, she thought drearily. Even now she could not be sure he was not hoping she would retract her determination to dispose of her money. It was not too late, for nothing could be done until she reached that fatal twenty-five years in a few weeks' time. All his fine words could not wholly convince her that he was unaware of that fact and anxious to conciliate her before she had given it away.

"I am no longer a Conde," he went on, looking at her steadily. "It is senseless to perpetuate a title without the lands belonging to it. I have become a simple Andalusian farmer."

That made her laugh. Rafael could never be simple.

"You look the same to me," she returned. "And to me you will always appear a great gentleman." She moved restlessly. "What are you trying to say? Are you having ... second thoughts?"

"I have never changed in regard to you."

"What precisely do you mean by that?"

"What I say." The velvet eyes regarded her intently.

"But you have altered. You say you will not accept your money, but possibly you do not need it. You have an air of affluence. You sit there in a couture gown. (So he had recognised it for what it was and it was misleading him.) You look extremely lovely, enough to turn any man's head, and you are about to become famous. You have a splendid future before you, and I can hardly expect an Andalusian farm could content you now."

"It might . . . ." She paused, glancing at him coyly.

"Domesticity would seem so dull to you after all this." He waved a hand indicating the chattering diners, the glittering glass and silver on the tables, the shining napery and the view from the window.

"This isn't my right setting," she informed him. "And the dress was a gift. I live very simply in an attic studio and when I eat out it's in small cafés."

She became silent, reviewing all he had said. Obliquely he had practically proposed again, but he had not yet said he loved her. Once, words of love had slid glibly off his tongue, inspired she had believed by his desire for her wealth, for she could not believe that then he had not had his eye upon her prospects, directed thus by his scheming mother.

"You say you've not changed, Rafael," she said gently. "But before you proposed, wasn't the money uppermost in your mind?"

He shook his head. "Not in *my* mind, but in mama's. You must not be hard on her; she was brought up to believe in marriages of convenience."

"Yes, that was obvious," Rosalie observed dryly. "She would not have tolerated me for a moment if she hadn't an ulterior end in view."

The black widow who had torn the veil of illusion from her eyes and shattered her happiness.

Watching her, Rafael asked, "Do you remember the occasion I offered you the position as my mother's companion?"

"Yes, very well, and very violent you were. I've always wondered why."

"I was being torn in two. I wanted you to stay, but I thought it would be better for you to go. When I took you to Las Aguilas, I believed you were a cheap little tart. I meant to avenge myself on you, after which I would have dismissed you with a trinket and contempt. But I was very wrong. You were spirited and provocative, but underneath you were innocent. No man had plucked my dewy rose, and I was ashamed of my intentions." He turned his head away. "I think I began to realize that before we had even reached the Castillo."

"Yet you put me in that vast bedroom and nearly scared me out of my wits."

"My *pobrecita,* you have much to forgive."

She gave him a mischievous glance. "It was quite . . . exciting."

"Was it, indeed?" His eyes glinted. "It is not surprising you give a wrong impression, Rosa. One might almost suppose . . . ." He broke off and looked at her intently.

"I'm still unplucked, as you put it, if that's what you're wondering."

"I was not," he denied swiftly, almost too swiftly, she thought.

"Your conventionalism distrusts artists," she told him. "You think we lead a wild life, but mine has been anything but that; just slog . . . and memories."

"I am glad you retained the memories," he said eagerly. "So they were not all bad?"

"Far from it."

"That is encouraging. But to continue with my story . . . explanation . . . what you will. I am trying to make you understand all the crosscurrents that governed my behavior toward you, which must have seemed to you so inconsistent, did it not?"

She nodded. "Especially the finale, if all that you've said is sincere."

"Every word."

"Then it was completely unnecessary. The break was caused by that stupid pride of yours, Rafael. I was too hurt to pick my words, but you could have persuaded me . . . ."

She looked at him reproachfully. So much pain could have been averted if he had tried.

The scene was fixed indelibly in her memory: the proud, cold man, counting out the extra money needed to take her out of his life, money she had since returned and he had never acknowledged, her bitterness and heartbreak.

"I think not. I may be proud, but you are stubborn, Rosa. As I have said, that money of yours was an obsession with you. Nothing I said then could have convinced you that my feelings for you were genuine."

She thought back, recalling her emotions at that time. The wound the Condesa had inflicted had been too raw to be easily assuaged.

"Possibly that's true," she admitted unwillingly.

"After I had presented you to mama, and she was sure she had recognized you, she became determined that I should marry you. She had intended to reinstate the family dignities with Consuelo's money; having lost that, she meant to get hold of yours. The companion idea was hers, she was certain you would jump at it. All the time she was urging me to make love to you, confident you would fall for my—" his mouth twisted "—experienced technique. It would not have been difficult, Rosa, because from the first when I met you in the road I found you desirable. But as I was beginning to have a very sincere regard for you, the whole scheme revolted me. I doubted if your happiness lay in a Spanish marriage—you would have had to give up your independence, your nationality and the career you were dreaming about, and I was ashamed to take advantage of your youth and inexperience. You saw me as a romantic figure, and if you felt anything for me it was only a young girl's infatuation. So though I wanted you to stay, I told you to go. But you didn't walk out as I expected you to do; you wished to delay your departure and threatened to go to the Guardia Civil unless I gave you compensation. I thought then that you were as calculating as I had been, and should you take the consequences of whatever might befall, I would not try to save you."

("*Bien,* I have warned you, so on your head be it." That cryptic sentence that had so puzzled her; the danger had been himself.)

"Then in Andalusia," he went on, "you seemed to fit in so well that I began to think that if I were patient I might win your lasting love and be able to make you happy. But I am not an impetuous boy to rush into an unsuitable union. Mama declared that you were ready to fall into my arms if I gave a sign, but I did not altogether trust her judgment. She was blinded by gold dust." He smiled ruefully.

"She despised me as a woman," Rosalie said bitterly. "She was certain I could not hold you."

"She told you that?"

"Not to my face. I overheard her talking to Señora

Carvello. She deplored the necessity of an alliance
with such a nondescript person as I was, and said you
would soon tire of me and go elsewhere."

"*Por Dios,* Rosa, she libeled us both!"

"I believed her, then. But what happened, Rafael?
What brought you up to scratch?"

"Luis Carbello. Mama warned me I might lose you
to him. She said you were tired of waiting for me to
declare myself. Then when I saw you together by the
swimming pool, some demon of jealousy entered me
and . . . well, you know the rest."

"Yes," she echoed, "I know the rest."

The rapture followed by swift disillusionment. She
could not risk such pain again, and she must be very
sure that this time Rafael was sincere.

"I shall have to think," she said slowly. "You see, I
have tried hard to forget you." She smiled wistfully. "I
wasn't very successful, but I have made a life of my
own."

"But you can still paint at the Casa Blanca. After
all, it was Spain that inspired your masterpiece."

And you, she added to herself, but that was an inspiration that would not come again. It had been born of
pain and renunciation as most great works are.

"I will not press you now," he told her gently. "I
shall be staying in Paris for a few days, but you must
give me a definite answer before I leave."

Rosalie was silent, looking out of the window. A
launch crowded with passengers went by, its brilliant
lights reflected in the slowly moving water. In her
mind's eye she saw the patio at the Casa Blanca, the
pattern of the vine leaves on the white walls. She had
been enraptured with the place, but would it have the
same appeal after this lapse of time? Rafael had said

that she fitted well into that environment, but that had been the old Rosalie, not her present more sophisticated self. Love would bridge all difficulties of adjustment, but did Rafael really love her, or was he merely seeking a companion in his loneliness?

A fair-haired girl at a nearby table rose to her feet, and seemed to be having some sort of disagreement with her escort. Her shrill petulant tones brought Rosalie's head around, and as she looked at her, she remembered Lucille Lenoir.

As the couple left the restaurant, she asked Rafael, "Where does the fair Mademoiselle Lenoir come into this? Isn't she offering you consolation?"

Under her eyelashes she watched him closely for some hint of guilt, but he showed none.

"She is staying at my hotel with her present, er, protector," he said coolly. "It was by chance we came into the exhibition together. I did not take her there. Her man, you see, dabbles in art, and he asked her to go and look at the pictures." Seeing the doubt in her face, he exploded violently, "*Madre,* Rosa, do you expect me to live like a cloistered monk on memories of what might have been? I am not an artist dedicated to a cold muse. If a pretty woman shows she likes me, must I repluse her?"

"She is pretty," Rosalie said slowly, wondering how far the affair had gone. "And is the picture dabbler complacent?"

"I have not tried to tempt his pretty lady to betray him," he returned sternly. "In fact, it is he who insists upon entertaining me, thus bringing us together. Paris is a lonely place without friends."

Rosalie felt ashamed of her suspicions, but before she could make amends, he went on, "Must we quarrel again and over such a trivial matter? It is you I came to Paris to find, Rosa. Did I not tell you that?"

"No, you said you had come on business that required your personal touch."

"Precisely. You were the business. I tried to forget you, Rosa, but it was not possible. You had got under my skin. Your memory refused to be exorcised." He looked at her anxiously. "But you, Rosa, are you hesitating because you have formed other attachments? I have heard your name coupled with the red-bearded artist whom you say you entertain in your studio, and painters have no morals."

"I'm afraid Jean's won't bear investigation," she said, laughing, "but I assure you I keep him at a distance. Of course I know that friendship between men and women is something you can't understand in Spain."

"We find it . . . improbable."

Rosalie played absently with the stem of her wine glass. Rafael was jealous of Jean, and certainly he was a jealous man. Jealousy of Luis had provoked him into his former proposal, but she did not want this new jealousy to provoke another crisis. Rafael's reappearance had awakened her old love for him, but he had made her suffer with his pride and arrogance. If he had told her all that he had told her tonight before she left the Casa Blanca, how much she would have been spared! If he was not an impetuous boy, she was no longer an impulsive girl ready to be submerged in her first experience of passion. She needed to be very sure before she submitted to him again, and if she married him it would be for always.

"Jean Duprez in only an artist colleague," she told him. "I don't care two straws about him."

He returned gravely, "I accept your assurance. You always were transparently honest, Rosa. As I said, I do not wish to rush you. You must think well and truly, for if you return to me, I will never let you go again."

As he spoke the last sentence, passion sounded in his deep vibrant voice, glowed, also, in his dark eyes. Fascinated, Rosalie stared at him, on the verge of surrender. But she need not do so yet. He had given her time and though she had little doubt of her decision, it would be pleasant to let him woo her, keep him in suspense a little longer, before she yielded entirely to his domination.

"Very well, Rafael," she said demurely, "I promise to do just that, and I won't try your patience too long."

He gave her a long considering look and Rosalie had to check an urge to tell him there was no need to wait. She was his, as she had always been, but he still had not said in actual words that he loved her.

He took her home in a taxi, and his hand sought for hers in the enclosing dark. She half feared, half longed for him to kiss her. If he did, it would be the end of her resistance, but apparently a taxi was too public for him with his Spanish propriety, to attempt such an intimate demonstration. She had to content herself with his firm handclasp, and she remembered with a flash of amusement Luis's description of the conventional Spanish courtship. He was allowed to hold her hand for three minutes in the cinema. Rafael held hers for much longer than that.

The taxi became caught in a traffic jam in the Place de la Concorde, but she would not have minded if it had stayed there all night. The fountains dripped golden rain under the bright lights, and the façades of the famous buildings and the central obelisk were floodlit. Paris was a city of magic to her that night.

As they neared Philip's apartment building, she said, "You will have to make it up with my brother, you know, if . . . ."

"I am prepared to do even that," he promised.

"Even that," she mocked him softly. "Implacable Spaniard, aren't you?"

"But you will teach me tolerance, *mi queridita.*"

Then they were there, and he was handing her out of the taxi and guiding her in through the door.

"I won't ask you up to my eyrie," she told him. "It's late and . . . ." She broke off, for she had been going to say, you wouldn't think it proper. But this was Paris, and perhaps Rafael did go up to girls' apartments. She did not know.

He said courteously, "It is late, and I must not keep the taxi waiting. Good night—*que deurmas bien.*"

Again he did not kiss her, and out of the tail of her eye Rosalie saw the concierge was watching them. Feeling deprived, she thought that he need not have minded that old man who must have seen many good-night embraces.

Instead he formally shook her hand, bowed and left her.

Up in her room Rosalie was too excited to sleep. She wandered about her studio looking at her half-finished canvases. Would she ever finish them now? She had told Rafael that any woman could marry and have a child, women who could not paint like she could, but it had been all bluff. As Rafael's wife and, if so blessed, the mother of his children, she doubted if she would still want to paint; if she did it would become a mere hobby.

The telephone rang. Rafael's voice.

"Are you in bed, Rosa?"

"I'm on my way."

"Fool that I am, I never fixed our next meeting."

"You said you were giving me time to think."

"That does not mean I am to be deprived of your company. I said I would not press you. Where would you like to go? The opera? The Moulin Rouge? Or perhaps a *bateau* on the Seine—I believe we can dine on board."

She decided upon the last. The next day promised to be fine, and it would be delightful to travel up the Seine through floodlit Paris; there would also be plenty of other people on the launch. Unless she meant to capitulate at once, she dared not be alone with him.

Less inhibited on the telephone, he poured out a flood of passionate Spanish, and Rosalie finally went to bed with his words of love still sounding in her ears and a glow in her heart. Rafael de Santaella had at last said he loved her.

THE NEXT MORNING Rosalie took Alex for a walk in the little park that was situated near the apartment house. She often did this when she needed a breath of fresh air, and Consuelo was glad that she should do so. Alex has passed his first birthday and was beginning to walk with waddling, stumbling steps and make sounds that were nearly words. He was very fond of Tante Ros. Rosalie wondered what language he would eventually speak—he was surrounded by Spanish, English and French. Probably a bit of each.

She sat on a bench with his stroller beside her, while he investigated leaves and stones that were scattered on the path, bringing each new find for her inspection with gurgles of glee.

It never occurred to her that Rafael might be prowling in the vicinity, hoping for a glimpse of her. She was dreaming of their meeting that evening and had decided that she would resist him no longer. Tonight she would tell him that she desired nothing more than to be his wife.

Alex was standing by her knees when Rafael came striding down the path. The child's chubby fingers were clutching her pants for support, while he babbled inarticulately and she supplemented their conversation with baby talk. Her face was soft and tender as she bent toward him. Soon, God willing, she would have a child of her own—not a replica of Philip's blond handsomeness, but a dark Santaella.

Rafael came to a halt in front of her before she noticed him. She looked up to meet a blaze of anger and incredulity.

"That is the baby you painted," he accused her. "He is yours, but you said you were not married."

Two pairs of gray eyes stared up at him in startled surprise.

Bewildered, Rosalie replied, "But I'm not." And then some imp of perversity entered her, a crazy impulse to tease him for his lack of trust in her, before revealing that Alex was Consuelo's son.

She said flippantly, "It is not essential to be married to have a child."

The instant she saw the change in his face, she realized what her misplaced levity had done. It was livid, the black eyes full of contempt. The word he hurled at her in Spanish was one she had never dreamed any man would ever call her. Then he strode away before she could speak. She called wildly, "Rafael!" but he did not turn, and was soon out of earshot.

She sprang to her feet, for she must catch up with him and tell him whose child Alex was. She dumped the boy in his stroller without waiting to fasten the straps and started in pursuit of the striding figure.

Alex gave a wail of fright and indignation, tumbled out of the stroller and tried to follow her. He fell flat on his face and his wail became a roar.

Rosalie stopped her headlong pursuit of Rafael. She must go back to the baby. He was her brother's precious son, the apple of Consuelo's eye. From the noise he was making he might be really hurt. Despairingly she glanced toward Rafael's rapidly disappearing figure and ran to pick up the child.

CHAPTER TEN

ROSALIE RETURNED to the apartment building hot, tired and in a vile temper. She had spent a futile half hour pushing Alex around the park hoping to come upon Rafael, but even while she searched, she knew her quest was in vain. He would have left, and by the time she finally gave up he could be at the other side of Paris.

Her vexation was with herself for her foolish tongue, which was so apt to say the wrong thing, mingled with resentment against Rafael for being so ready to think ill of her. But in the present instance she had to admit he had some justification. Out of a mistaken sense of tact, she had not mentioned Philip's son when she had dined with him. He had noticed her pictures of the baby, and Alex did bear a strong resemblance to herself. And Alex looked so very English that it would not occur to him to connect the child with his dark Peruvian mother. Later he might possibly arrive at the truth, especially if some mutual acquaintance happened to mention Philip Smith's offspring, and since the Pas heirs were so much in the news, that was quite probable. But he might leave Paris at once in disgust and go back to Andalusia to find solace with his herds and horses.

He had never approved of Rosalie's independence and was suspicious about her relationship with Jean Duprez, and in spite of her assurances, seemed to imagine that she led a wild Bohemian life.

"If mother and Philip had curtailed my liberty and surrounded me with duennas and chaperones, he would have believed in my virtue," she thought savagely. "As if virtue is worth anything if it hasn't been tested!"

But Spanish men had so little faith in female virtue that they took care their girls were not tested, and if she had led a cloistered life, she would never have met Rafael at all.

Poor Alex was crying by the time she started for home. He sensed his Tante Ros was upset and felt somehow to blame, as innocently he was. Nor during her frantic tour of the park had she given him any attention, he who was not used to being ignored. He felt neglected and abused and set up a roar for "Mum . . . ma!" as they entered the vestibule. His vocabulary extended that far.

Rosalie perfunctorily tried to soothe him, but he sensed that her thoughts were engaged elsewhere and continued to wail, as she carried him upstairs. Consuelo's French *bonne* met them at the entrance to the apartment, and the infant doubled his howls.

"*Le pauvre, il est fatigué et il a faim,*" the woman said, for Rosalie had returned much later than she usually did, and the woman did not altogether approve of these morning outings.

"*Tais-toi, mon ange,*" she went on. "Oh, *mon Dieu!*" She had discovered a faint bruise on the child's forehead, which Rosalie in her preoccupation had not noticed.

Hearing the commotion, Consuelo came running to find out what was wrong, and Rosalie was treated to a display of Latin emotion that could not have been greater if Alex had broken a limb.

Pleased with the uproar he had created, Alex ceased to wail, gave a loud chuckle and subsided into thumb-sucking satisfaction.

Consuelo handed him over to his nurse, who took him away to be fed.

At last able to make herself heard, Rosalie explained that he had fallen down when trying to run, which was not unusual, and Consuelo apologized.

"He tumble often," she said. "It would not be your fault." Rosalie winced because it had been. "Do not look so guilty, *querida*. I am sorry I—what Felipe say—blow my top. You know how precious he is to me."

Rosalie agreed that she did, and sighed. She would never have one of her own now.

"All's well that ends well," she observed. "So long, Con. I'll take him out again tomorrow if you can trust me with him."

"*Claro,* but are you in any hurry? I have that which I wish to say to you."

Reluctantly Rosalie entered the salon, which Consuelo had indicated. She was longing to go up to her own room and face her despair in solitude, but having jeopardized Consuelo's infant, the least she could do was to listen patiently to whatever her sister-in-law wanted to confide to her.

Motherhood had increased Consuelo's exotic beauty, and she fairly glowed with an inner radiance. She was wearing a well-cut dark red suit, calf-length, with a white lace blouse, for she never wore trousers and dressed to emphasize her feminity. Rosalie, in her trousers and knitted top, looked like a slender boy beside the other's opulent curves.

The salon was beautiful; Señor Nuñez had furnished it for his daughter's wedding present. The wide chesterfield and armchairs were upholstered in black, against pale panelled walls. The carpet was white, the curtains black and white. The somber effect was relieved by the brilliantly colored Spanish shawl thrown over the piano, which Consuelo sometimes played, and a woven Indian blanket over one arm of the chesterfield. The tall windows filled the room with light, and on small ebony occasional tables were crystal vases filled with roses and carnations. Over the mantelpiece that housed the electric heater was one of Rosalie's pictures, one of Alex crawling across a green lawn, his head raised to watch a passing butterfly. It was the only picture in the room.

"Felipe has had the story accepted by the magazine," Consuelo told her excitedly. "He has the thrill as great as if he had found a gold mine."

"Well done, Phil!" Rosalie exclaimed. "I'll congratulate him when I see him. May it be the first of many." She glanced at Consuelo, who was looking a little embarrassed. "Was that what you wanted to tell me?"

"No. Please sit down, Rosa." As Rosalie seated herself resignedly on the chesterfield, she went on diffidently, "I have been told Don Rafael de Santaella called here for you last night. I was much surprised. I have not told Felipe yet, but I do not think he will be pleased at all."

Rosalie felt the hot color flood her face at this wholly unexpected attack.

"It was due to Phil's thoughtlessness that I encountered the Santaellas," she cried indignantly. "As I told you both, I was dismissed from the *parador* because of Phil, and if the Condesa had not offered me a job, I should have been in difficulties." For this was the story she had told them. "So I don't see why Phil should mind if Don Rafael is so kind as to look me up," she added defiantly.

"I only thought . . . well, he cannot feel friendly toward Felipe," Consuelo observed. Scared of the Conde herself, she mistrusted his motives for turning up in Paris.

"He has forgotten about all that."

"Oh?" Consuelo did not look pleased by this information. Believing herself to be the heroine of an elopement drama, it was disconcerting to learn that the deserted bridegroom had forgotten her.

"But, Rosa *mia,* do you like him?" she asked in some bewilderment.

Rosalie said simply, "I love him."

"*Madre!*" Consuelo stared. "I know he is supposed to be very attractive, though I could not see it; but then he frightened me, so cold and so aloof." She gave Rosalie a sly glance. "But perhaps he is not so with you?"

Rosalie blushed again, and Consuelo looked troubled.

"You do not think . . . it is your money?" she asked hesitantly.

"I did," Rosalie said grimly. "That is why I left Spain, but now he insists that it is not."

"So now I understand," Consuelo cried triumphantly. "Felipe said when you come back, you changed much, and that fierce dedication to your painting—it was not natural. I should have guessed. All your pictures are of Spain, and that one I do not like, it was of Don Rafael. *Queridita,* I am so glad. Marriage is the only true happiness for a woman, where there is love. So he comes to Paris to find you? You make it up, and now you will be so happy."

"I'm afraid not. You see he turned up in the park this morning when I was out with Alex, and owing to a silly thing I said, he's gone off believing your son is my child."

"I always say Alex is more like you than me," Consuelo began, then she did a double take. "Oh, no, no, Rosa!" and then suddenly they were both laughing helplessly.

"But cannot you explain?" Consuelo asked, as her mirth abated. "I would not like my *chiquillo* to ruin your life."

"That's the awful part about it, Con. I can't put him right because I don't know where he's staying and Paris is a big city. Besides, he may have rushed back to Spain in a rage."

"Then you would know where to contact him, but it would be a long way to go," Consuelo pointed out. "But would not anyone else know where he stays?"

"There was that cabaret dancer he brought to the exhibition—Lucille Lenoir—but I don't know where she is appearing, if she is appearing, which she probably isn't," Rosalie said despondently.

"A cabaret dancer?" Consuelo asked dubiously.

"Oh, he explained about her," Rosalie said offhandedly, knowing well what Consuelo was thinking. She herself felt a qualm. Would he go to Lucille for consolation, and was their relationship really as innocent as he had declared? She pushed away the unworthy thought. If she could not trust Rafael's word, she did not deserve him; it was only the reputation he had earned, probably much exaggerated, that made her suspicious. Unfortunately she had that morning destroyed all his trust in her.

Consuelo was saying, "Perhaps an advertisement in *Le Matin*?"

"I don't expect he reads a French newspaper, and what would we put? 'Come back, I'm not the baby's mother. Rosa.' Oh, Con, I've always been in a false position as far as he is concerned. At first he could not understand how any respectable girl could come to Spain to serve as a waitress. He thought I was an easy pickup and. . . ." Rosalie stopped and flushed, realizing she was betraying too much. Not for the world would she like Consuelo to know the true story of her entry into Las Aguilas. She had a low enough opinion of Rafael de Santaella without that.

"But if he engaged you as a companion for the Condesa he cannot have thought bad of you," Consuelo remarked.

"Oh, well, he soon found out his mistake," Rosalie said hastily.

"And fell in love with you? How romantic! But does he know you have refused your dowry?"

"Yes."

Consuelo expressed the doubt that had occurred to Rosalie.

"Then was it really Alex who drive him away, or was it . . . ?" She hesitated, unwilling to wound her companion.

"The discovery that I'm no longer an heiress?" Rosalie finished for her. "He declared that it made no difference, but he may have had second thoughts."

Consuelo nodded sadly. From her experience of Rafael de Santaella, she could not credit that he would accept a penniless bride.

"Oh, well, it doesn't matter now," Rosalie said resignedly. "It's all over, and perhaps it's just as well. I don't think I'd ever make a good Spanish wife."

"You are too independent," Consuelo agreed. "You

would have to live his life, you know. That is how it is
with us."

Rosalie sighed. She had decided that to live Rafael's
life would be no great hardship, not if he truly loved
her. Last night new and entrancing vistas seemed to be
opening before her, but now she was back to square
one.

"Thanks for trying to help, Con," she said with
assumed lightness. "This love affair of mine is
doomed. We don't seem able to avoid misunderstand-
ings. I'd better get back to my easel and start another
picture. 'The Forsaken Mermaid' would be a good
subject—no, I'm wrong, it was the forsaken merman,
but I don't feel inspired to paint Rafael with a fish's
tail. What the . . . ?"

Heavy footsteps sounded along the passage outside
the door, followed by a noisy altercation, and Rosalie
thought she recognized the voice. Surely he would not
dare to intrude here?

Consuelo's maid had pushed the door ajar in some
agitation. *"Pardon, madame,"* she gasped. *"Voici un
monsieur—"*

A stentorian voice interrupted her.

"Cut the trimmings! Rosa, are you here? The concierge said you came up." Jean Duprez strode into the
room. "Out!" he commanded the maid, snapping his
fingers.

The girl scuttled away with relief.

"Really, Jean," Rosalie remonstrated. "Your manners are appalling. This is my sister-in-law's home.
You've met her?"

"At the exhibition. Your pardon, beautiful
madame," he grinned at the astonished Consuelo. "I
must speak with your *belle-soeur tout de suite.* What
has happened is too ludicrous!"

He began to pace the room with rapid strides, to the danger of Consuelo's occasional tables with their vases of flowers.

"Sit down, Jean, before you break something," Rosalie besought him. "What can be so urgent that you have to burst in here like a tornado?"

He stopped in front of her, his red beard bristling.

"Me, I have been challenged! I have been insulted by your dispossessed one—he looks exactly like your picture, so I conclude that he sat for it. I would not have minded if what he said was true, but I am not the father of your baby. I am quite sure you have never had a baby; the baby in your pictures is yours, *madame.*" He bowed to Consuelo. "I may be an old *roué,* but I am not that untidy!"

Rosalie began to laugh; then as his full meaning struck her she stopped and stared at Jean.

"You mean Don Rafael came to the exhibition and accused you of being the father of a nonexistent child?"

"*Oui,* Rosa, and I demand an explanation. You know I adore you, but I will not be used to make another man jealous!"

Rosalie began to laugh again and it was Consuelo who asked the relevant question.

"Where is the Conde de las Aguilas now?"

"The how much? I have no use for titles, nor, he tells me, has he. Monsieur de Santaella, after drinking a pernod with me, is downstairs in the taxi we used to come here, waiting for me to locate you, Rosa. It seems he had some delicacy about intruding upon Madame Smith. . . .Rosa, are you going to faint?"

"No, but how did you convince him? Let me go to him."

She started toward the door, but Jean stopped her with a firm hand.

"*Restez ici.* After being threatened with a cut throat—*alors*, perhaps a black eye would be more correct—I deserve to arrange matters my way. *Naturellement*, I deny this unexpected paternity. The *bébé*, I tell him, is Mademoiselle Rosa's nephew. She is, alas, of virtue unassailable, and if anyone says otherwise, he must deal with me, Jean Duprez. So we go and have a drink—two drinks, and I bring him here to apologize. But lest he harbor any lingering doubt, and I think that one has a very suspicious mind, and we will, with your concurrence, *madame*—" he again bowed to Consuelo "—give him absolute proof. If you will send for the *bébé*, whom he will recognize, he shall see it in his mother's arms. I will contrive a picture most *charmant*. And you, Rosa, shall appear as your great poet says, as chaste as ice and pure as snow, or is it the other way around?"

Rosalie looked at Consuelo apologetically, saying, "This man's a lunatic. You don't have to do what he says, or receive Don Rafael."

But Consuelo's Latin love of drama was greater than any lingering antipathy toward her former suitor. Pressing the bell beside her, she announced, "I will receive him for your sake, Rosa, and I will send for Alex."

When Rafael was brought into the salon by a triumphant Jean, and from his expression he did not appreciate the artist's method of conducting his affairs, Consuelo, with Alex upon her knees, looked the picture of maternal beatitude.

Smiling graciously, she held out her hand to him, saying, "Welcome to our poor home, Don Rafael."

Rafael's eyes had gone straight to Rosa, and he gave her a rueful smile, but at Consuelo's words he turned to her and kissed her hand with courtly gallantry.

Jean let out a great laugh. "And now Rosa's," he said.

"In Spain an unmarried girl does not rate a kissed hand," Rafael said stiffly. Then he smiled. "But a *novia* may, I think, be saluted, even in company."

He moved toward Rosalie and lightly touched her cheek with his lips.

"Oh, *mon Dieu*!" Jean exclaimed. "Take her outside and do it properly. But before you go, do you want the taxi or can I have it?"

Rosalie glanced out of the window through which the spring sunshine was streaming.

"I think a walk in the park would be nice," she said demurely. "Shall we let Jean take the taxi, Rafael?"

"Anything to get rid of him," Rafael agreed. "But I would like to see that studio of yours, where I am told—" he glanced at Jean "—no man alone has been permitted entrance."

Amid Rosalie's paints, palettes and half-finished canvases, Rafael did kiss her properly.

THE CASA BLANCA, and a man and a woman who had come through many vicissitudes to a close understanding and fulfilment of their love.

On Rosalie de Santaella's wrist was a bracelet, not the ill-fated diamonds, but a much lighter one of linked gold, and on the third finger of her right hand—for this was Spain—two rings sparkled. She lifted a glass filled with manzanilla, the wine of Andalusia.

"To us, Rafael, on this the anniversary of our wedding day."

Smiling, he lifted his own glass and drank.

"Any regrets?" he asked as he put it down.

"None whatever."

A faint anxiety showed in his eyes as he looked at her glowing face.

"But you have not painted a picture since we were married."

"Later, maybe," she told him unconcernedly. "But so far I've simply had no time. I've been fully occupied learning to be a good Spanish wife, and next year, I'll have still more to do—all being well."

"You mean . . . ?"

She bowed her head. "Are you pleased, *señor*?"

Rafael took her into his arms.

"My cup of happiness was full," he murmured, with a tremor in his voice. "But now it is overflowing."

As Rosalie raised her mouth to meet his kiss, she knew that she had found her true destiny.

And there's still *more* love in

Harlequin Presents...